The Time the Waters Rose

&

Stories of the Gulf Coast

The Time the
Waters Rose

&

Stories of the Gulf Coast

PAUL RUFFIN

The University of South Carolina Press

© 2016 University of South Carolina Press

Published by the University of South Carolina Press
Columbia, South Carolina 29208

www.sc.edu/uscpress

Manufactured in the United States of America

25 24 23 22 21 20 19 18 17 16
10 9 8 7 6 5 4 3 2 1

Library of Congress Cataloging-in-Publication Data
can be found at http://catalog.loc.gov/.

ISBN 978-1-61117-614-8 (paperback)
ISBN 978-1-61117-615-5 (ebook)

This book was printed on recycled paper with
30 percent postconsumer waste content.

Grateful acknowledgment to the following:
Arkansas Review: "Islands, Women, and God"
Boulevard: "The *Drag Queen* and the Southern Cross" and "The Time the
    Waters Rose" (under the title "The Time the Rains Came")
California Quarterly: "Devilfish"
Louisiana Literature: "Mystery in the Surf as Petit Bois"
Louisiana Literature Press: Excerpt from *Pompeii Man*
Pembroke Magazine: "*Cleo*" (under the title "The Boat")
Texas Short Stories II: "The Hands of John Merchant"

For Amber, as always

The sea, once it casts its spell, holds one
in its net of wonder forever.

Jacques Cousteau

Contents

Preface

I was brought up in rural Mississippi, where fishing was usually a pleasant experience with reasonable expectations: You went after a certain kind of fish with certain baits, and you knew that what was at the end of your line lay within those expectations. It would be only so long and weigh only so much, and it would look right, the way a fish ought to look.

Only an occasional water moccasin or loggerhead turtle represented a threat, and they were easily dealt with, usually by removing their heads one way or another and making them wish they had chosen an easier meal.

I married into deep-fishing shortly after I earned my PhD from the Center for Writers at Southern Mississippi and for over thirty years spent several weeks a year on the Coast, primarily in the Moss Point/Pascagoula/Gautier area.

My father-in-law owned a twenty-five-foot Cobia, *Sundowner,* which we took fishing out on Petit Bois and Horn Islands and the deeper water beyond them several times a year. We fished the surf, we fished the wrecks, and sometimes we went all the way down to the Chandeleur Islands off the Louisiana Coast.

Some nights we would wade in the surf for flounder, looking for that faint outline of a flatfish lying just below the sand waiting for prey.

Some of the most interesting times for me were when we would rig the boat for shrimping and drag in the Sound, pulling in an incredible range of sealife. I would hold up one strange fish after another, and my father-in-law would patiently name it and tell me all about it. (I'll never forget the day I held a little elongated oval fish out to him and asked him what it was. "It's called a cunt cover," he said, without elaboration. I was more careful with future inquiries.)

No matter how many times I went out into the water of the Gulf, I never failed to sense the mystery of the sea, which has served up its secrets to man since the time that he discovered it and will continue as long as he ventures into it. This is the way it has always been and always will be, and it is good.

The stories in this collection all celebrate in some fashion the mysteries of the sea, and most are drawn from experiences I had along the Mississippi Coast, a lost time now but a long way from forgotten.

The opening story is a crazy thing I started when I was ten or twelve years old and suffering the interminable Sunday sermons I had to live through in an Assembly of God church near Columbus, Mississippi. The preachers were *called* to spread the Gospel—*called* meaning that they did not have to trouble with earning any sort of degree to prove themselves worthy of entering the ministry. All they apparently needed was a memory sufficient to recall the high points of their sermons and the oratory skills required to rattle off platitudes to support them.

They told the same old Bible stories the same way year after year, leaving me simply dying to hear about three dumbasses riding into Bethlehem on donkeys, bearing goat-horn rattles and wool blankets for the Baby Jesus, maybe a grass-stuffed doll covered with rabbit skin. I wanted Moses to sashay out there in the mud and pick up baskets of fish and then have the walls of water engulf him, just before a big-ass whale came along and swallowed him—just see how well *he* would handle it. Let ol' Lot turn to a pillar of salt, name him Morton.

In time I began writing these stories to suit myself, and I can promise you that not one of them turned out the way they were supposed to. The Noah story was one of them.

One day a couple of years ago I was sitting at the computer recalling some of those old Bible stories I wrote, and I got to thinking about how much fun it would be to finish the story on Noah. Which I did.

Yeah, I know that it's not a Gulf story, but it does have saltwater in it, big-time, and it has some rednecks doing what rednecks do long before they were invented. As Flannery O'Connor once said, every story should have some humor in it, some leavening agent. Most of these stories are downers to one degree or another. The Noah story was meant to be fun, so don't be offended—enjoy it.

Paul Ruffin

The Time the Waters Rose

I knew the minute the wild-eyed sonofabitch hobbled up to the house babbling about how a great flood was looming on the horizon and that we'd better get ourselves right with the Lord and help him build this big Goddamn boat that he was just nuts. And the wife said so too. We had seen him the week before downtown in front of the bakery up on a barrel yelling at folks to listen to him about God's warning to the wicked of the world. Kids was throwing donkey turds at him and yelling, but he went right on ranting about the great flood that was coming to wash away the slime from the Earth.

"Two of every animal there is?" she said when he had shuffled off into the dark.

Hell, he could barely walk. I didn't know whether he was drunk or just old and tired, but I sure couldn't fancy him building a boat big as he was talking about and herding a big bunch of animals onboard and taking care of 'm. He didn't look like he could do much more than take care of hisself.

"What he said," I told her.

"That's the first I've heard of it. And if anything's on the wind at all, one of the women in my mohair quilting club woulda said something about it. They got their nose in everything. So-and-so's fourth cousin by his third marriage got knocked up by a shepherd over in Ajalon and you can bet we'll know about it before she gets her first round of the morning sickness."

"I don't 'spect there's anything to it, but I'll walk over to Baruch's place tomorrow and see what does he know about it, if anything. I ain't seen a thing posted anywhere about heavy rains coming, but it wouldn't surprise me since I just got the crops in on that hillside. Gonna wash everthing away. Like I'm worried. It ain't rained here in . . . let's see. . . ."

I held the light over to the calendar and flipped back a few sheets, and sure's shit, the last time I had recorded any rain was nearly six months ago. It's the driest damned place on Earth. Flood, my ass. Rain ain't ever done much more than make a little mud in this hellhole.

"But, Hiram, he said we could drown if we don't do what he says and hep him with that boat. Ark—that what he called it?" She was scrubbing the bottom of a pan with some salt and making so damned much noise I could barely hear her.

"Yeah, Ark," I yelled at her over that racket she was making.

"And where's he gon' get all them animals at?"

"Hell, woman, I don't know. He was kinda secretive about that. He just said that the Lord would provide."

"Then why don't He provide him a boat?"

"Or just keep the rain away," I said.

We didn't talk about it anymore that night. I had a lot more than that to worry about, what with the worst case of the piles I'd ever had. Ass burned like it had a nest of mad hornets shoved up it, and nothing in the house but candle wax to cool it down. I told her I'd find out more about the flood business the next day in town. If didn't anybody there know, I'd walk over to Eben and see could anybody over there tell me anything. It was a little troubling, the way the old man's eyes sparked when he was talking about that boat.

Baruch was setting on a wine keg under an olive tree whittling on a new walking stick when I came up. He went through two or three a year. Rough on'm is what. He hadn't been right since he fell off a camel a few years back and probably never would be again. And when I talk about right, I don't mean just the way he walked. But he wasn't bitter about it.

When I asked him about the Noah guy and his notions of a coming flood, Baruch just grinned and twirled a finger at his right temple.

"Aw, hell, Hiram, that loony's been talkin' about a flood for might near a year now. Him and them boys of his. He prolly got the notion from his daddy, Lamech, that died a few years back—made it to almost 800. Hell, Noah's 600, if he's a day. He ain't been by here, but his middle boy, Shem, I think his name is, give my wife a damn flyer a few weeks ago."

"A flyer? What'd it say?"

"Same shit he's been tellin' everbody: There's a flood comin' to wash away the wicked from the face of the Earth, and we need to get our hearts right with God and help him build a big boat—a ark, he calls it—to haul us and a whole bunch of animals around until the water goes down. I just thowed it in the fahr."

We chatted on awhile about the weather and olive futures and stuff, and then I walked on in to Hazar to have me some lunch and see what did anybody know there about the coming flood.

Didn't nobody in town know anything for certain, just what we already knew. Malachai the Barber said a bunch of kids finally ran Noah off from in front of the bakery four days in a row before he finally give up and started going door to door to talk to people. Said he hadn't heard nothing more than what I had about it, and I figgered that if a barber hadn't heard anything else, there *wasn't* anything else.

I still went by the Post Office, though, which is where people mingle a lot and post stuff on the boards. Three old men were playing checkers just outside the front door, but they didn't have anything to add, so I went on inside and found a couple of the flyers that Baruch had mentioned, but that was all.

The postmaster, a guy by the name of Kish, was busy bitching on his usual subject: how if we all had two names, his job would be so much easier sorting the mail.

"Ever sumbitch in the world, I rekkin, has got just one name, and we have run *out* of'm. I got five Moseses and four Nathans and Malachises, three Ruths, and it gets confusing as hell. If everbody had two names, it would just about get rid of all this mess, but noooooooooooo—one name is all we go by. Somebody comes in here looking for his mail, and we gotta set down and sort it all out. 'Let's see, you the Moses that lives on Paradise Lane. No? Dusty Lakes Plaza? No? Oh, so you're either the one on Dry Well Road or Sand Flea Acres or in that shack over by Tickle Cunt Creek, which ain't had enough water in it in twenty years to tickle a damn instep.' Like I say, it gets to be confusing as hell. Someday they's gon' be a law passed about it, and everbody'll have two names, or maybe even three, and my job will be a whole lot easier. Likely I'll be bad dead before they get around to it. Don't nobody ever think about people like me that's got to deal with crap like this.

"And they all bitching at me about *delivering* the mail to'm instead of them having to come pick it up, lazy turds. Like I got nothing better to do than load up my donkey with a sack of damn mail and haul it out there to'm. I guess the day'll come for that too."

When I managed to ask him about Noah and his warning, Kish started in on the name business again.

"I got *three* Goddamned Noahs. The loony you talking about is so fuckin' blind that he don't get much mail anyhow—the women have to read it to him—so I just got two to fool with on a reglar basis, thank the Lawerd. And, no, I don't know shit about no flood a-comin' and sure as hell don't pay no attention to that old fart."

He was still mouthing about it when I left.

I had me a piece of cheese and a bottle of noon wine and hitched a ride with an old man with a cart full of watermelons headed over to Eben, which is a bigger town a couple of miles down the road. There was a guy there that was pretty good at predicting weather, and I figgered that if anything big was coming, he would know. I mean, I had plenty to keep me busy at the house without running around all over the place chasing a rumor, but old Noah did sound convincing.

Reuben's his name, the guy in Eben, and he runs a little weather station out of his house. Got a barometer and wind vane and all kinds of thermometers hanging on the walls, but the funny thing is that the instrument he pays attention to most is a little of piece of wood with a twig on it he's got nailed to the mantle. He explained it to me one day.

"You see how that little limb is drooped down, like it's sad and give up on the world?"

I nodded.

"Well, when rain is threatenin', it rises up like the biggest hard-on you ever had."

"A woody?"

"Yep, a woody. Stands right up there, tall and proud, and you better get ready—they's rain a'comin'."

When I asked about Noah's prediction, he snickered and said that he'd heard all that from several people that come by to talk to him about it, but the peckerometer said that there wudn't no rain coming anytime soon. He said, in fact, that he hadn't seen it with a hard-on in right at six months.

Well, that was gospel enough for me, so I set out for home, taking a shortcut through the hills. I liked walking back through there because it's real high, and you can see for miles and miles in all directions, and the trail is almost as smooth as the road. In places you can look down and see both Eben and Hazar and the whole road that stretches between them. I liked seeing people and donkeys and carts creeping along like lazy ants moving from one bed to the next. One time I seen a couple in a cart pull over on an orchard road and get completely naked and lay down with each other on a blanket. *My* peckerometer predicted a hard rain that day.

There's a well about halfway along the trail, so I stopped by for a drink and said howdy to a couple of old women who were filling their jugs and washing out some clothes. It bothered me a little that they had underwear and socks hanging right there on the lip to dry, where they could drip right back into the well, but I just pulled up the bucket and dipped me a drink with the gourd and kept my mouth shut. I saw no reason to mention the Noah thing to them, just nodded bye and left.

Something I didn't know but found out that day was that one of the places that you can see from the high trail is Old Man Noah's spread. I had seen it quite a number of times walking up there, but to me it looked like any other sorry-ass dirt farm: a couple of run-down shacks and sheds with sheep pens and goats and scattered olive trees and usually a bunch of kids running around naked.

When I seen that damned curved beam running what must have been half a hundred long steps, with ribs coming up from it all along one side, and a dozen stacks of timbers towering nearby and a whole bunch of people swarming around chopping and sawing and hammering, there wasn't much room left for guessing—somebody down there was in the early stages of building a mighty big boat. Guess who, my ass.

So, though it wasn't clear whether ol' Noah knew what he was talking about or not concerning the weather, it was damned clear that he intended to build an ark.

And that got me to worrying. Noah wasn't known to be a wealthy man, but most folks considered him to be pretty wise—I mean, in six hundred years you gotta pick up a lot of useful knowledge. If he talked all them people into helping him with the boat, then it was clear that *somebody* believed him. Of course, they could have been all famly and were just humoring him. Whatever, I was determined to check it out the next day.

The next morning, early, I told my wife I was going over to Eben to try to find out more about the threat of a flood and headed out along the road for a bit, then cut up through a field and on up through the rocks till I got to the hill trail. It was just the right time of year for a journey, the ways easy, the weather warm, the very dead of spring—I almost felt like writing a poem. But I didn't.

About halfway up to the ridge, beyond where the trail lay, it occurred to me that I ought to have brought somebody with me, just to confirm what we were seeing, in case it came to that. Baruch came to mind, but crippled as he was, I decided that wouldn't work. He'd bitch every inch of the way and then pout and not be willing to take notes or anything to help me out.

So I settled on Uriah, a guy I had known since we were snot-nose kids, who lived just half a mile or so from the road, but on the other side.

I wore my ass out hoofing it over to Uriah's place, only to find him another half a mile over in a field shearing some sheep. Or at least that's what I thought he was doing. Let's just say that he was paying very special attention to the animal he was with, but the instrument he was using wasn't shears.

It's not that I blamed him. The bitch he was married to weighed in just shy of the heft of a camel and had lips just about as big as one. And a hump. Just one. And in the wrong place. Meaner than anything else alive, the best I could tell. Drooled snuff. Farted a lot. And she was pure-dee mean. If she had been my wife, I would have had to kill her a long time ago. Or just left. Or she would have killed me.

At any rate, I squatted down and let him finish—no sense in ruining the day for him—and when his robe was right and he felt good about the world again, which was obvious from the happy tune he was whistling, I stood up and walked on over to him.

"Hey, Hiram. Didn't see you coming," he said.

He left hisself open with that, but I just said, "Wasn't sure it was you back here, but I guess it is."

I didn't have time for small talk, so I just up and asked him had he heard about the great flood that was coming, and he laughed and said yeah he had, so I told him about seeing the

skeleton of the ark that ol' Noah had started out and asked did
he want to see it. And he said yeah, he did.

It didn't take us but a couple of hours to get to where we could
look down on Noah's place, and I gotta tell you, however many
folks they had working on it, they had made some progress. The
ribs were up on the other side, and they had beams along the
top and a few laps of planking up from the bottom. We could
see all that from the ridge, but what I wanted was to get down
close and see who all that was helping him out and get a notion
about how the hell they were gonna build the thing that it could
handle all them different kinds of animals. I mean, you got two
of every kind of animal there is, some of'm are gonna wanna
eat some of the others, so you gotta have some way of keeping
them separated. You know?

What I suggested to Uriah was that we slip down through the
rocks and underbrush and crawl up as close as we could and
have a good look at things. He was still feeling good from the
romp in the pasture and said whatever I wanted to do was fine
with him, so off we went.

It took just over an hour, I'd say, judging from the sun, to get
close enough to where we could just about see and hear what
was going on, and it wasn't an easy trip. I was half tore up from
briars and sharp rocks, and so was Uriah, but that was the price
we had to pay for being snoopy. We hunkered down and shared
a piece of goat cheese and some bread I had shoved down in a
pocket and peed and then made the last few yards of the crawl
to where I could make out who was doing what.

Best I could tell, it was Noah's clan all right, ever damned
soul clambering around on that ark. The old man hisself was
lording over everybody, the way I knew he would, leaning and
looking and criticizing and then showing'm how it ought to be
done. You can't do that kind of thing to anybody but famly and
keep anybody around.

Not five minutes after we got situated, he got impatient with some kid with a hammer and took it away from him and started driving a spike, but he did a mislick and hit his thumb, and I ain't never heard a God-fearing man yell like that before.

"Goddamn it to hell, sonofabitching motherfucker!"

Everbody just stopped what they were doing—sawing and hammering and measuring—and looked up at where he was standing on the ladder with his thumb in front of his face. I couldn't tell whether it was bleeding or not.

Then he turned his face up to the sky and yelled out, "Why have I got to use *gopherwood*, Lord? Why the hell—how come I can't use something softer, something that you can drive a Goddamn—something you can drive a nail thoo without busting your hammer and thumb and without using a thousand God— a thousand strokes to finish the job?"

Didn't nobody laugh. I guess when a 600-year-old man that has the inside scoop from God about a coming disaster loses his cool, you just take it in stride. But he wasn't finished.

"And why in the hell—why have we got to measure all this shit, all this stuff out in cubits, which ain't the way our rulers are calibrated? That shit—that stuff went out over 200 years ago. Cubit, my ass. They teachin' different stuff in the schools these days, but nawwwwww—You gotta make me use cubits on this fuc . . . on this boat."

He mumbled something else, but we were too far away to hear him. After he was through ranting, he crawled down off the ladder and went over to where a couple of his grandkids or great-grandkids, or whatever the hell they were, were looking over some plans. By the time you are 600, I figger that you kinda lose track of the grandness and greatness of any of your offspring and treat'm all like dogshit.

And that's the way he seemed to be talking to all of'm. I never heard him do a thing but bitch the whole time we were hunkered in the bushes.

"That ain't right, boy. Can't you saw a straight line?"

"Bend ever Goddamn—ever nail I got, you weenie!"

"Naw, that room you drawed ain't gonna be big enough for no damned rhino, much less two, and they gotta have room to hump and lay down!"

"You can't put no fuck—you can't put no giraffe on the lower decks, fool, where they gonna put their heads at?"

"God—uh, shit, uh, shoot, Barak, you can't put no square beam in a round hole."

"You can't put rats next to the snakes, Jethro—they'll be eat up before we rise up off the chocks."

"Levi, I have told you that the women won't be able to piss through them tubes that you boys are gon' use—you gotta have somethin' for them to squat over."

"No, Goddamn—no, Hamram, you can't take that slut with you, even if you did knock her up. She ain't in the fambly, she ain't gettin' on the boat."

On and on he went. I knew we weren't going to remember all of it, and I started to ask Uriah to write some of it down but remembered he couldn't write. And I didn't have anything to write with or on anyhow.

At one point the old man clambered down from one of the deck beams and walked over nearly to where we were hiding and set down on a rock and started praying.

"Why me, Lord, what have I ever done? I ain't responsible for the heatherns on this Earth, and I don't think it's fair for You to lay all this on me. I got eighteen boys working for me, and all of'm together ain't got sense enough to pour piss out of a wine jug, with the directions wrote on the bottom, or build a sheep shed or donkey cart, much less build a boat big enough for all them animals.

"And how, by the way, am I going to be able to round all of'm up, them animals? Some live thousands of miles from here, and I am 600 years old and can't walk that far, much less herd a bunch of animals—even a *turtle* can outrun *me*.

"And how am I gon' pair'm up? Apes and elephants and zebras I got no trouble with, but how about snakes and armadillos and ants and stuff like that? How I'mon sex'm, Lord? If ain't nuthin' hangin' down, how I'mon know? Muskeeters? Lizards? Turtles? Ants? I just don't know enough about their equipment to know how to pair'm up. I might screw up and ruin their chances down the line, Lord. It's a heavy burden.

"And, Lord, ain't nobody takin' me serious. I got kids thowin' donkey turds at me and callin' me all kinds of names in town, and everbody's laughin' at me."

By and by he got to blubbering so that I couldn't make out even half what he was saying, but it was obvious that he didn't feel totally prepared for the mission the Lord had laid on him. Finally he just wept a little and then got up and pissed into the bushes and went back over to the ark and commenced to bitching again at the poor bastards working on it.

Me and Uriah watched a little while longer and then eased back to where we could get up and walk through the bushes and rocks to the ridge and then on home. Ever once in a while we'd stop and look back down at the ark. It is surprising how much work that many men can do in a few hours even when they don't know nothing about how to build the boat they are working on. I don't know shit about boats, but I can tell you that the size of that damned thing was impressive. One thing for sure I knew: If a flood *didn't* come, there wasn't no way they'd ever move it to a body of water big enough to float it. Have to turn it into a bed-and-breakfast or burn it. I was just glad it was them down there and not us.

On the way back me and Uriah talked it all over and decided that we wanted to know more about when Noah expected the flood to come, since the old man was obviously convinced that it *was* coming. Again, you gotta believe that a man 600 years along has been doing things right or he wouldn't have made that long a haul and still be able to climb a ladder and swing a hammer. Whether he had any kind of direct line of communication with

God or not remained to be seen, but I figgered that he might. So I just told Uriah that I was gon' go down there the next day and talk to the man hisself and see what could I learn. Uriah said OK, he'd go with me.

Well, the next morning, bright and early, Uriah showed up on my doorstep raring to go. Said what he wanted most was to see the ark up close, even closer than we had, and learn how the hell ol' Noah intended to lay it out for that many animals and how he would feed and water'm and get rid of their shit and how he planned to get'm there in the first place.

This time we just took the road over to Noah's. It was a nice day, not a cloud in the sky, and I just couldn't imagine that there was enough rain coming to flood the valley. Our feet threw up little puffs of dust every time we took a step, and our tracks would stay right there in that road until the wind covered them up with more dust. I would have bet my balls on it.

Well before we came in sight of Noah's place, we could hear hammering and yelling, and when we got closer, we could hear the rasp of saws being used to cut planks out of those big timbers that were stacked all over the place. I don't know where in the hell he got that many pieces of gopherwood, whatever the fuck it was. I remember thinking that it was awfully yellow-looking, almost orange on the ends, and I gathered from all the bitching about it that it was real hard to cut and drive nails and spikes through. Hell, timber was hard enough to come by anyhow in the valley. Most of the trees were either olive trees or runted cedars, big enough for fence posts but not much more. I guess he had it hauled in from somewhere. Or God just dropped it down outta the sky.

But if that was the case, why didn't He just drop off an ark, already loaded with animals? Or better yet, call off the damn flood. There were a whole lot of other ways to deal with the wicked. You know, plagues and shit like that. Or turn'm all into homosexuals and they'd die off eventually.

I didn't have time to worry on that anymore because in a few hundred more paces we were looking up at that monstrosity. Hell, I thought it looked big from the bushes we were hiding in yesterday, but standing in the shadow of it gave me a much better idea of what size boat ol' Noah had in mind. I didn't doubt that it could hold two of every kind of animal in the world, with plenty of room for provisions for them and the people that would be onboard.

Nobody seemed to pay us the least bit of attention until Noah hisself walked out of the house and over to where we were.

"Howdy," he said. "Can I hep y'all?"

"Hey, Noah," I said. "You was by the house the other evening talking to me and my wife about the flood that's coming. And that boat."

"It's a *ark*. And, yeah, I remember you. Who's he?" He nodded toward Uriah.

"My friend Uriah. We just wanted to drop by and talk to you some more about the flood and ark and all."

"Uriah? Oh, yeah. You wudn't home when I dropped by your place, but your wife was. I hope you don't mind me a-sayin' so, but that's one mean bitch. She thowed a jug of piss on me when I didn't get off the porch soon enough to suit her."

"Yeah, she's too fat to leave the house to piss or crap, like the rest of us. Just uses a jug. I 'spect that's what she had."

"I don't know *who* the piss come out of, but it sure as hell come outta that jug, and it sure as hell hit *me*. Even the dogs wouldn't come near me when I got home."

"Well, I—"

But Noah cut him off. "Y'all come on in the house and set a spell."

A couple of minutes later we were sitting at a table in his kitchen, which was just bustling with women and kids. When we walked in, they were apparently getting together food for the boat hands for lunch. Mounds of bread everywhere. Cheese. Meat of some sort, probably goat. Jugs of something, water maybe. Whatever they were doing, they turned from it and started whipping up some breakfast for the old man, who wolfed down bowl after bowl of what they handed him, washing it down with something from a tall clay jug.

He didn't look at us or say anything while he was slurping down whatever the hell it was. Looked like whey, with flecks of cheese in it—he was real sloppy with it, and it sloshed all over the front of his robe, which was already stiff with something white and flaky. There was sawdust in the creases too, and streaks of some kind of oil slung out across his chest and shoulders.

In a bit, he threw back the last of the stuff in the jug, set it down with a thud, and belched so loud that everybody in the room turned and looked at him and laughed. And he laughed too. So did me and Uriah, once we figgered that was what we was supposed to do. Then he wiped his mouth with a sleeve and leaned forward on his elbows. Behind him the women and kids went back to what they were doing when we come in.

"What more do you want to know about what I have been trying to tell the whole damn valley about?"

"Well," I said, "I guess that we need to have some kind of proof that what you say is so. I mean, it ain't rained here in over half a year, and we don't generally get but a couple of inches a year, at best, according to that guy Reuben I talked to over in Eben that has got a weather station set up in his house."

"I'll take God's word over Reuben's. And I know him. Knowed his father too. The fact that he relies on a wood peter to predict rain ought to tell you everthang you need to know about *him*."

"Mr. Noah," Uriah said, "all we want's a reason to believe that a big flood's comin', you know. My two kids ain't never even played in a puddle of rain water. One of'm ain't even *seen* rain."

"I am 600—"

"Yessir," I said, "I know that you're 600 years old, but that—well, frankly, Sir, it don't make you an authority on floods."

"I never said I *was* an authority on floods. But God has kep' me alive all these years for somethin', and that somethin' was to save the world's creatures from certain destruction from a Godda—from a flood, and them that don't believe it and get on the boat with us is gon' drown, sure as shit!"

"Now, Poppa," one of the women cautioned. Didn't look old enough to be his wife. Couldn't been over a coupla hunderd.

"This is my house and my table, and I am 600 years old, and I can talk any damn way I want to!"

"PawPaw Noah," a little girl said as she eased up beside him, "you not sposter take the Lawerd's name in bane."

The old man smiled and patted her on the head. "I didn't, sweet thang. I almost did, but I caught myself."

She crawled up into his lap and leaned her head against his shoulder, right in some of that slop from his breakfast. It was disgusting is what.

"PawPaw, Noah. . . ."

"Yes, sweet child?"

"What about the tortoise?"

"Tortoise?"

"Yessir, the one that had a race with the hare. We read about it at school."

"A hair? I know what hair is"—he reached down and tugged one of her locks—"but I don't know what a tortoise is. You gon' have to explain it to me."

"Oh, PawPaw, you a mess is what. You jokin' me. A hare is kinda like what you call a rabbit, and a tortoise is some kinda turtle. They just call'm differt in school."

Then she told us the whole story, which apparently Noah had never heard.

When she finished, she looked up at him with tears in her eyes. "I was wonderin' what will happen to the tortoise if the hare hears about the flood and don't dally like he done in the story and runs off and leaves the tortoise to get drowneded."

"Child, the turtle will get here just fine. *And* the rabbit. The Lord will pervide."

"Besides," I put in, "a turtle lives in water most of the time anyhow, so he won't care one way or the other."

The old man leveled his eyes at me. "That may be, but I got a spot set aside for a couple of turtles, whatever they call'm in school. There will be turtles on the boat."

"PawPaw Noah. . . ." A little boy had wormed his way up on Noah's other knee.

"Yes, child?"

"What about the polar bears?"

"Polar bears?"

"Yessir. Them big ol' white bears that lives up in the cold country where there's ice and snow all over. How they gon' make that long trip and get down here on time?"

"They just gon' have to hurry is all. The Lord will pervide."

"Are you gon' let skunks onboard, PawPaw Noah?" the little girl asked.

"And buzzards?" The little boy's eyes were almost as big as the plate Noah's goat cheese had been on.

"Ayup, they's a place for all of'm. The good and bad and purty and ugly. Gon' save'm all."

"PawPaw Noah, where we gon' do-do and pee at, over the side of the boat?"

"Naw, son, We got pee pipes on both sides of the deck, and I got a outhouse at the very back of the deck that hangs out over the edge. Everthang'll drop right down in the water. Got plenty of rolls of real soft leather to wipe with too."

Then he gave the women a signal, and they shooed the children away from the table, and we got back down to the business of the flood.

"How come," Uriah started, "how come we ain't got some general word from God about no flood?"

"Because the Lord don't talk directly to just *everbody* is how come." He motioned for one of the women to fill his jug again with whatever the hell it was he was drinking. I got a whiff of it every now and then, and *I* damn sure didn't want a swig of it.

"How come to you then?" Uriah was getting a little bolder.

"Because I am 600—"

"Everbody on the God-d-d—everbody on the planet knows how old you are, Noah," I said, "but how come He chose *you* to spread the word. How come He ain't give some general sign somewhere, like . . . like . . . I don't know, a burnin' bush or something or a big star in the east, something everbody could look at and know it was God sending a message?"

"How'd he get the word to you anyhow?" Uriah asked.

Noah give him a stern look. "He just did is all. I ain't got to tell you everthang that goes on between me and Jehover. He give me the Word, and I been spreadin' it the best I can. My legs ain't what they was a coupla hunderd years ago, so the famly's helpin' me out. We told everbody we could, and if they don't believe, that's their prollem, not ours. A flood is a-comin' and I am buildin' a ark, and that's all there is to it."

He gave us another real stern look.

"And them that ain't on the boat when it starts to float are goin' to be drowneded."

He stood and leaned on his fists. "And, now, if we're thoo here, I'm gon' get back to supervisin'. We ain't got long to finish this thang."

That was it. He turned around and shuffled out the door, trailed by five or six kids, and the women just went right on working like we wasn't there. So I motioned toward the door, and me and Uriah left.

We discussed the flood business all the way home and didn't come one half a cubit closer to a decision about what to do

than we had before we went over there. I had a cup of wine on
Uriah's porch—his wife was slamming shit around inside, so I
was fine enough with the porch—and then went on home to tell
my wife what we didn't find out.

As the weeks wore on, I took to the high trail every couple of
days. I could tell a lot more about what was happening from
that vantage point than I could even in the bushes where me and
Uriah had hid that day. I tell you, them ol' boys was flat slapping
some wood on that ark. The ribs were completely covered over
by the time I saw the boat again, and they were working down
inside the thing, where, of course, I couldn't tell nothing about
what was going on.

The slowest part of it, it seemed to me, was sawing out
them damn planks. They'd wrestle a beam around with the
help of some jackasses and lift it up on some sawdonkeys, and
sometimes it would take might near a dozen men to heft the
thing. Then two men would latch onto a cross-cut saw, with one
man on each side of the beam, and they'd work their way down
a line the length of it, one pulling and one pushing, and almost
ever time it take'n nearly a hour to get all the way to the other
end. Some kid with a bucket of olive oil on each side would
splash a spoonful on the top and bottom of the blade ever few
strokes. It ain't many jobs tougher than sawing gopherwood, I
kept thinking.

I also kept thinking that if the Lord delivered all them damn
beams, why the hell didn't he already have'm cut into boards. A
lot of what was going on didn't make any sense to me.

Two or three weeks later, they started laying on the upper
deck, which took almost a week to finish, what with all the
planks they had to cut. Next they started on several little houses
on deck, with window openings covered by wooden flaps that
open and closed.

I couldn't see what was going on on the other side of the
ark, but they fooled around over there for several days. One

afternoon Uriah slipped in on the backside of Noah's place and eyeballed that other side, and he said they'd made a great big door that dropped down and formed a ramp, and we decided that that had to be how they were going to get the animals on.

Me'n Uriah didn't talk much about the ark and coming flood for three or four weeks. He was busy working his sheep, whatever that happened to mean on a particular day, and I had a hell of a bunch of olives to press. All that time the weather was the same as it always was: clear and bone-dry. Not even a cloud the size of a man's big toe. Dust everywhere. Sand all over the house, tracked in by both of us but blamed mostly on me. My wife might drag in a couple of shovel loads of grit with them long damned outfits she wore that some called a tunic but I called a tent, but never under the light of the sun or dark of night would she admit to dirtying up the place. Rain, my ass. I found myself *wishing* for a flood.

Still, there was something in the way the old man talked about the coming flood that led me to give it a little more serious thought. He said it could all start any day now, so I figgered I might just head on over and talk to Reuben in Eben again to see what did the peckerometer have to say about it.

I took the high trail on the way over so that I could get a good look at the ark, and I gotta tell you, there was flat some activity going on down there. Apparently they had finished the boat and were in the process of loading it with supplies. It looked like a line of ants stringing out from the outbuildings and main house, everbody carrying big boxes and bags of stuff around to the other side and up the gangplank, I guess, then coming back around and heading in for another load. Noah was running about like a wild animal, his robes flapping, yelling orders to his workers, all still famly, I figgered, though I wasn't sure. Ever so often he'd cock his face toward the sky to the west.

All that let me know that he had a host of believers, even if they were famly. It was enough to get me to thinking serious again, so I decided I'd go on over and talk to Reuben and see what did *he* know.

Just as I was sliding down out of the rocks to get on to Eben, I happened to look off toward the east, where there had been a little cloud of dust for a bit, and lo and behold, there were two big animals of some sort just coming out of the cloud, and they looked like something I'd never seen before—long necks and legs but too far away for me to tell what color they were. In another minute or so, two other animals came in behind them, these big and bulky and low to the ground. The ark was about to take on animals.

Now I was thinking even more seriously than ever about what was happening down there. I mean, wasn't nobody herding them animals—they acted like they knew what they were doing, and what they were doing was heading directly toward that damn ark.

Then I literally ran on over to Eben and went directly to Reuben's place after getting me a slug of water at the well in town. Wasn't nobody talking about rain.

I found Reuben in his weather shed hunched over some charts, and he was so into whatever he was doing that I half scared the crap out of him when I came through the door.

"Lord God," he said. "You need to knock before you come in on a man."

"The door was open."

"So it was."

Well, I saw he was real busy, so I just up and asked what did his peckerometer have to say about the weather.

He grinned and pointed. "Never seen my pecker act like that."

The little limb was straight up, almost parallel with the trunk.

"I've had that sumbitch right at twenty years, and it ain't ever behaved like that."

"I take that your pecker predicts rain."

"My pecker says we might ought to get on that boat. I been lookin' over records from as far back as a hunderd years, and there ain't never been no rain in these parts this time of year that amounted to much more than a spit. But my pecker says some is coming, and probly a lot of it."

I had a cup of goat milk with him and asked what he intended to do, and he said nothing, unless it really cut loose, and then he was gon' snatch up his bitch—meaning his wife, I figger—and head for higher ground.

Well, hell, the only thing I knew to do was get on back home and see what my *wife* wanted to do. The kids were grown and all gone and could fend for theirselves, so it wasn't but two people I had to worry about.

She didn't have to think about it long. Even after I told her about Reuben's special instrument and what it said, she was dead set on staying right where we were and let the old fool go on and wear hisself into the grave working on a big old boat that, like as not, would rot right there on the chocks or sit there as a monument to human folly for a thousand years.

Two mornings later I woke up to thunder. I mean, it was rattling shit around in the kitchen. By noon rain was slashing across the roof and driving so hard against the windows that they were leaking all over. My wife just set to mopping up and bitching about all the dust and sand in the house turning into mud. I swear, she would fret over ashes on the kitchen floor with the house burning down around her.

It rained and rained and rained. Straight through the day and night, and no letting up at all. Solid sheets of the stuff. What Uriah would call a turd floater. And it didn't stop the whole damned week. We were trapped in that house bitching at each other over the least little thing. When you been married over thirty years, it ain't easy to get along in the best of times, much less when it seems like the whole damned sky is dumping on you and you are trapped in a little house breathing each other's farts.

On and on it went, and by the end of the week I was beginning to have second thoughts about ol' Noah and his boat.

When by the middle of the next week the damned rain was still hammering down, I got to thinking that I might go over to Uriah's and see what did he make of it all. I was just about convinced that Noah was onto something. I had seen more rain in a week and a half than I had in all the rest of my life, plus some.

So I asked did she want to go with me, and she said no, she'd keep mopping up all that water and then scrub out the mud when the rain quit. See what I mean? The end of the damn world might be coming, and all they think about is mopping up the water and mud in the house. When I went out the door, she was down on her hands and knees squeezing out rags into a bucket.

The going was hard, I'll tell you. When you live knee-deep in sand and dust all your life, you got no idea what it's like to deal with that same depth of mud and water. I got to thinking about ol' Noah, living 600 fucking years in dust and sand and now. . . .

I lost my sandals so damned many times in that sucking slop that I finally just tied them together around my shoulders and slogged on barefoot until I could make out Uriah's house, which stood on a little rise. Water was already a couple of feet deep out from the front steps.

Uriah met me on the porch. I could hear his wife whining and bellowing inside, and he seemed awfully glad that I had dropped by. He went back in briefly for a jug of wine and slammed the door behind when he came back out, like he was trying to keep a wild animal in its cage.

We set down on the edge of the porch and finished off the jug while his wife raged behind the door.

"Man, I gotta tell you, that woman is driving me crazy. Cooped up in there with her for might near two weeks . . . Jesus, I had almost decided to just go ahead and drown myself and be done with it."

"Looks like you wouldn't beat it by much, the way the water's coming down. And up. I'm not even sure I can get back home. What you think we oughtta do?"

"One thing's for sure—we gotta get to higher ground. I been watching that water creep up on us, and it's gon' be on the porch in another few hours. And I'm talking about me and you, not that crazy hag in the house. She can drown, far's I'm concerned. The kids are staying with her momma up in the mountains across the valley, so I guess they'll be OK way up there."

"What you think, then? Head up to the ridge?"

"I'm thinking yeah, go up there and at least get a good idea what's going on. The whole valley's gon' be flooded soon."

"What about heading over to Noah's and see can we get on the boat?"

"*If* we can get over there," he said. There's some low spots between here and there on that road."

"You wanna try?"

He glanced back at the door, behind which the witch was throwing things around and yelling ever foul word I'd ever heard.

"Bet your ass I do. I wanna be anywhere but *here*."

So he ran back inside, grabbed another jug of wine, and slammed the door behind him. His wife was banging something against it.

"Just stay here and drown, you Goddamn whorin' *bitch*!"

He slogged out to where I was waiting. I wanted to be out of range of anything that woman might throw from the doorway.

"I wouldn't mind saving a sheep or two, but I don't give a dead camel's ass if she drowns right there. I'll tell you this much—if ol' Noah let that slug on the boat, I'd just go on and wave bye-bye and drown."

"But I guess you'd save your irresistible ewe, huh?"

I guess I lost him on that one. Or he just ignored me.

That water was up to my waist by the time we got to the main road, and I knew right then that there wasn't going to be no way we'd get to Noah's place following that route—we'd have to go on the high trail and get as close as we could before dropping down again.

Getting to the trail itself was damn tough. Dragging my robe through that filthy water took all my energy, and Uriah wasn't doing any better, what with that jug of wine that he was lugging, and there was shit floating all over the place, bushes and limbs and boards, snagging on it. At one point I thought about just shucking it and then realized I didn't have anything on underneath, and showing up at Noah's nekkid in front of the women might not set too well with the old man. Could keep me off the boat. I figgered Uriah didn't have anything on underneath either.

It must of took two hours to get to the foot of the trail, which normally would of took less than half an hour, but finally we made it. Before we started up to the ridge, we decided to polish off the jug of wine, which we did in short order. It felt a whole lot better in the belly, Uriah said, than it did having to lug it in the jug. It sure made the going easier as we headed up the trail.

I looked back from time to time at the spread of water below us and finally accepted the fact that whether or not there was a flood coming that was going to wash away the wicked from the Earth, there was damn sure one already floating away everything that wasn't tied down in the valley. So whether that old bastard was totally right or not, he was right enough to put the fear of God in *me*. Once you drag your robed ass through nasty water up to your armpits, you get the message.

We couldn't see Uriah's house from anywhere along the trail, but I could see where my house should of been, and it wasn't. That dirty-ass water stretched out as far as I could see. I could imagine the hell my wife went through as that water rose and rose and rose in the house, and finally she had to have just give up and grabbed onto something and floated off. At least I hoped she did. At least she had to of been glad that the sheds finally got cleaned out, something she'd been on my ass for years to do.

I mean, she wasn't a bad woman. She just wore thin, the way women do after a long time of marriage. And I don't mean thin in body—she wasn't quite the heft of Uriah's bitch, but she would render enough to keep a famly in lard a couple of years. But enough of that. I figger her opinion of me wasn't much better. I just hoped she found something to grab onto and float. She was, after all, the mother of our children. And then I got to worrying about them.

Quite a bit before we got to where we could see Noah's place, we came to the realization that the big road wasn't there anymore—it was just water, water, water, and the rain was still coming down. It came in gusts, though, so one minute we couldn't see much more than a jackass's length in front of us and the next we could make out details down in the valley.

What we noticed most was that there wasn't anything *to* notice: The valley was totally flooded. From time to time we would spot something that we recognized, like a particular rock outcropping or the tip of a tree, and once we saw a couple of people clinging to a pile of timber. I was surprised that we didn't meet anybody else on the high trail, but we were still quite a way from Hazar and a lot farther than that from Eben. Still, it looked like some of them people living in the valley would have made it up there by that point. But, hell, me'n Uriah barely did. Nobody in this part of the world knows a whole lot about floods. I guess that you don't really learn much about one until you're in it, and we damn sure were.

In a little while we came to a peak that give us a better view of the valley, and then when we looked out, we could see where everybody was at. It looked like ever soul for miles around had gathered on one point of land—men, women, children, dogs—and it was clear enough why they was in that particular spot. Old Noah's ark was anchored a few hundred yards out, where him and his family seemed to be trying to rig their sails. I figgered none of them had ever been in a boat before, much less one that required anything more than a paddle, and it was obvious that whatever directions the Lord had give him for building the boat, He left out the chapter about sails.

We could see a lot of people floating around the ark, hanging onto logs and timbers and doors, anything that would keep them from drowning, and they were begging Noah to let'm come aboard. Some of them would even try to hang onto the side and claw their way up, but gravity was against them, and there wasn't a handhold to be had.

Then, lo, somebody threw a rope with some kind of grappling hook on it, and it caught on the railing, and the next thing we saw was this guy hauling hisself up, arm over arm, toward the deck. Well, the people on deck saw it too, and somebody went over and whacked him on the head with a board and he fell back to the water. They pulled the rope on board.

While we were standing there watching, high above it all, a couple of other people tried the same thing, but they got the same treatment and lost their ropes in the process. It was obvious that Noah'nem had the upper hand and wasn't nobody gon' get on that ark that wasn't already on it.

Me'n Uriah hung around awhile watching the spectacle and then decided to go down amongst the crowd and see could we find anybody we knew. We did and we did.

On up in the afternoon we gathered about us right at a dozen guys, all kin to some degree, and met up on the ridge in council, I guess you'd call it, to discuss things. The water was still rising, and we were getting squall after squall, so it was a matter of time before the water would cover everything, us included. The poor bastards down by the water's edge were backing up, and it looked like them that had been trying to get on the ark had give up and floated on back to shore. Somehow we had to get on that boat.

One of the guys had lugged along a couple of loaves of bread and a wine bag, so we decided to go on and refresh ourselves before getting down to business, which we did. Hell, none of us had any idea when we'd get our hands on bread again, much less wine, since ever damned place in the valley was underwater that would have had either. Anything the people had lugged up on the mountain with them would probably be gone by morning. By the middle of the afternoon we were all buzzing a little from the wine and, if not full, at least not starving to death. We set to planning.

"Rope," somebody said, "we need lots of rope."

"Which I know where we can get it at," said another.

"And grapplin' hooks," the first one said.

"Where we gon' get grapplin' hooks at?" Uriah asked.

"You can make a grapplin' hook outta any damn thing," I said. "Pieces of wood, tree roots, anything that'll snag up on that rail."

Uriah snorted. "You seen what they done to them that tried that."

"True." I nodded. "But what if we come at'm from four directions."

The others nodded. We'd all been thinking the same thing. I mean, all but Uriah, who was rarely involved in anything that required thinking.

"Go get the ropes," I said to the one that knew where there were some. The rest of us will round up something for grappling hooks. We'll meet back here at dark."

Coupla days later, me and Uriah were up on deck, feet propped on the rail, finishing off a rack of ribs.

I held up a rib bone. "What was that again?"

"*Yak* is what the sign on the door said. Hell, I don't know whut one is, but it's fine eatin'."

"And they took just the male, right? And the female was prolly pregnant?"

"Hell, he's had'm on the boat for might near three months, since they was loaded a long time before the waters rose, so don't you figger the old boy knocked her up in that length of time? If he ain't done his binness in that long, he probly never would have. Trapped in there with nuthin else to do, day and night. And, yeah, ain't nobody touchin' no females."

I kept thinking about how long it would have took Uriah to have nailed any female in one of the cages, but I kept my mouth shut. I silently thanked the Lord that didn't nuthin come of a human, animal coupling. I mean half rhino, half Uriah? Lord God. . . .

"What're Noah and his bunch saying about all this?"

"Well, you can hear'm raisin' hell down there in the bilges, but we left'm alive, and they get plenty to eat, even if it ain't the best cuts. You get hungry enough, you'll eat zebra horns."

"Zebras don't have horns," I told him.

"Well, hoofs then. They got hoofs."

We sat there awhile in silence then wondering what kind of exotic meat we were having tomorrow. I mean, good Lord, we had a hell of a menu to choose from. Gorillas, every kinda deer you can imagine, jungle cats, elephants, snakes. Eat the males and hope like hell they done their job before we eat'm.

I kept trying to rerun the whole thing in my head. It was sheer genius for us to float out there in the dark and throw grappling hooks from all four directions, a few seconds apart. We picked up another few hands to help us, but most of the people that had been standing watching the ark had headed on up into the hills. It was still raining like hell, and thunder drowned out the sound of the hooks. We were on that boat before Noah and his boys knew what hit'm. It helped that the old man was dead asleep below deck and the three imbeciles out on deck on watch were dead *drunk*. We had them on the deckboards in no time. It was bad to have to kill a couple of'm and throw'm overboard, but, hell, we give'm a chance to surrender.

The next step was to figger out where the other men were, which was easy enough—we just follered the snoring. We didn't know how lucky we were until later, but ever damn swingin' dick that wasn't on watch had a big bash in their dining hall and was drunk out of their minds. We tied'm up, one by one, and stashed'm in a big empty animal cage and chained the door. A couple of times I seen a door open and a woman's head stick out, but nobody said anything, so we just locked off the lower-deck stairwells and chained the doors to any rooms that seemed to have people in'm. We could deal with them later. When they got hungry enough, we could manage'm.

We could have throwed all of'm overboard. The first time we found land, we'd chunk'm overboard and let'm swim for it. Any of the women that decided to stay with us could. Hell, three or four of'm was already beggin' to join us. I figgered that in another couple of days, we'd let'm. I mean, you get horny on a Goddamn voyage, you know.

Stashed ol' Noah and his boys in the bottom cages that we moved the animals out of, with hay to sleep on and buckets to relieve theirselves in. Fed'm and watered'm twice a day. Yeah, it was dark and smelly down there, but it wouldn't last forever. Put the women and kids on the deck above'm—fed and watered them three times a day and let'm use the regular facilities, which wasn't much, but better than them damn buckets. They got blankets too. You just take better care of the women and children, since most of them was there against their choice anyhow.

When the sun come up that first morning, we signaled that anybody on land could swim on out and we'd take'm onboard, and a few folks come, mostly women and children. Like I say, most of the people had headed to the high hills way off in the distance.

"I wonder how God's lookin' down on all this?" Uriah finally quit sucking on his yak bone long enough to talk. "Rekkin ol' Noah's still in touch with Him?"

"Don't know. Don't care. I figger that if God didn't want us to take over the boat, He wouldn't have allowed it, and He ain't done shit about us butchering the animals and roasting them on deck. Lord, what a party every night! And we got months and months of fresh meat down there and more water and wine than we could drink in a year. If He didn't like what happened, He sure as hell didn't do anything about it. So I figger we're OK. Noah's famly and the pregnant females of every kind down there will survive, and that's what He wanted. That's what I figger is all I'm saying."

"Well, I hope to hell you're right." Then he reached down and fetched another rib off the platter. "You realize, though, we might not of thought this thing through. What if them pregnant animals have female babies?"

"Uriah, Goddamn it, we cain't be responsible for everthang!"

"Hey, guys," a voice came out of the dark behind us. "Reindeer roast OK for tomorrow night?"

"Oh, yeah, Lum, that'll be fine. Rice and gravy?"

"You got it."

"Thanks, man," I said. Then to Uriah. "It's amazing how one minute you're preparing yourself for drowning, and the next minute you're eating and drinking better than you ever have. Lord, what a life."

"Ain't it so?" he said. "Ain't it so?"

After a few minutes of silence Uriah said, "Onliest thing bothering me is whut about them sails. We know less about'm than Noah does, which ain't a whole lot."

"Sails for *what*? Where would we be sailing to? Some kinda damn foreign port? Hell, far's I'm concerned, we can just anchor this damn thing right here till the waters go down. Then we get on with our life. Main thing is to wait out the flood, which I figger we can do."

We had another round of wine, which ol' Noah had laid in in huge quantities, more than fresh water, and sprawled back to study a bright spot in the night sky. It hadn't rained in hours and hours, and Uriah swore what we were seeing was the moon trying to shine through. Could be.

One morning a few weeks later, I woke up on deck and saw the strangest thing either of us had ever seen. It was plumb clear above us, and to the north, where the clouds had moved off to, this great big old curved thing formed across the sky, like the bottom of a bowl, and I saw just about every color I had ever knew about in it. They wasn't any land showing anywhere—I wondered what the hell happened to all them people that went back into the hills, but, hell, we *tried* to save'm. I nudged Uriah and pointed it out to him, but he was already looking at it, with his mouth hanging open.

"Whut in the hell do you rekkin that is?"

I shook my head. "Damned if I know."

"Do you rekkin it's some kind of sign?"

I shook my head again and leaned back onto the deck and watched the damn thing stretched from one horizon to the other. Several of the others saw it too, so we didn't just imagine it.

Later that day we gathered up all the rope and rigged an anchor out of our made-up grappling hooks and slid it over the side. Eventually it bumped the bottom and took hold, so we tied it off and settled down to ride it out, however long it took, and it took a whole lotta days, I'll tell you. I didn't keep track, and I don't know that anybody else did, but it was a loooong time we bobbed around in all that water before we seen land again.

The food was damn fine, though, and there was plenty of wine, and in less than a week most of the women had come around to our side and paired up with some of us. Me'n Uriah didn't end up with one, which was fine with us. Hell, we were too old to think about having to deal with another woman. The main thing was that our meals got better and better, and the deck was cleaner, and it was damn cheery with children running around again and the sound of female voices.

Once the weather broke for good, ever morning we awoke to a blazing sun that danced off the ripples that stretched off forever in all directions, not a speck of land anywhere, and figgered that the flood had done what it was supposed to do, whatever that was, and the only thing to do from that point on was wait for the waters to recede and see what came of all this. At some point somebody went down and talked to the old man about what would happen, and he told'm that the waters would keep going down and at some point a white dove would come bearing a green twig and that would let everybody know everything was OK. We didn't know whether he got that from God or just made it up, but from that point on we kept our eyes on the skies, looking for doves. None of us had any idea what kind of mess we had made of God's plan by taking the ark away from Noah and eating a good many of the animals, but, then, we also figgered that if He let us get away with it, He must of wanted things to come out that way.

Then, lo and behold, I was stretched out on one of the deck chairs beside Uriah when I seen a speck way out over the water, and I watched it fly directly for the ark. Damned if it wasn't a white dove, which I had never seen that color of before, and he had a stick in his mouth with a couple of green leaves on it. He flared and landed right in front of me on the rail and just stared at me a few seconds, then dropped that stick at my feet, and I swear he winked at me. Then he was gone. And Uriah slept through it. I leaned down and picked up the little stick and nudged Uriah and showed it to him. But he wasn't impressed, just went back to sleep.

The rest of the story is routine enough, so I won't worry you with how things finally dried up and we went about our lives again. Just this: I ended up married to one of Noah's granddaughters that was only 150, but she looked like a spry 90, and we had three kids, named Leaha Naomi, Zilpa Ester, and Obadiah Hiram—you know, to help out the new guy down at the post office. I even tacked on a second name for me, Hiram Earl. Me'n Ester May, my wife, been thinking about coming up with a last name . . . on account of you never know when that kinda thing can come in handy.

Devilfish

It was like most days that we fished the wreck or section of pipe or whatever it was lying fifty feet below us that attracted snapper and grouper and kept our freezers full. A diver friend once offered to go down and see exactly what it was in that blue-green deep, but we argued no, it was better to imagine a twisted shrimper or storm-breached snapper boat where more sea life swarmed the decks than the men who once walked them would ever have believed. A snarl of net or piece of dredging pipe might satisfy the fish—not me and Sam.

It was the mystery of it that hooked a fellow—an almost religious awe—not knowing what lay in the sand beneath you or what was taking your bait way down there, not knowing its color or shape or size, whether it had two eyes, each on a side, or two on one side, or one eye or none at all. It might weigh in ounces or in tons. There was a lot I didn't know about what swam down there and what it swam around.

Sam and I were brought up inland, fishing rivers and creeks and farm ponds, where what jiggled your line was sure to be no heavier than a country boy could lift with one arm, no longer than the length of your leg from the knee down. Familiar as family, ordinary shapes, with an eye on each side and the colors right—predictable. And no more dangerous than a cottonmouth, which you just whipped at the end of your pole until his body snapped off from the head, or a loggerhead: You slid that big ugly sonofabitch up on the bank and bashed his shell with a rock or stick until it split and his guts spilled out and left him there for the crows. Momma wasn't into turtle soup. I know that sounds cruel about the turtles and snakes, but that's the way it was done.

The Gulf was another world for us, when we finally got there, Sam a few years before me when he took a job with the big shipyard at Pascagoula. I came later, after my college work, took a math teaching job at a high school not far from where Sam lived. He got married right away and had three kids before he was twenty-five, all gone now and married, with kids. I still batched.

Once we were there on the Coast, where we could look out every day and see that water arching over to the horizon, it drew us like a mistress. It was a rare weekend when we weren't out on Sam's boat, a twenty-two footer, anchored off one of the islands fishing the surf or, better for our freezers and tables, hauling up snapper and grouper from the wreck. But it wasn't just the fishing that kept us out there—it was the sense of mystery, of the unknown. Like I say, it was almost like religious awe.

I guess Sam explained it best one day when we were pulling a small shrimp net behind the boat, catching a few pounds of shrimp along with all kinds of fish and trash. He stared at a big pile of seething sealife we had just dumped on the pickboard, then up toward the pale disk of a daymoon off over the sea and shook his head.

"It somehow don't seem right to me for us to be looking around up there for little green men or whatever"—he gestured toward the moon—"when most people on this planet ain't got the foggiest notion what we got right here."

He raised his raking fork toward the Gulf, stretched out like a silver lid to the horizon, then pointed to the pile on the board and fell silently to separating the confusion of colors and shapes into squid and stingrays, crabs and fish of every type imaginable, lumps of mud, beer cans, and the handful of shrimp scattered among them.

This was just another snapper-hole day, one of twenty or so we had each year. We popped a couple of good-sized ones no sooner than the boat stabilized its swing on the anchor rope, the way we always did, but the strikes slacked off except for the bait-snatching of triggerfish and spades. No more gunwale-slamming tugs. But these lapses were normal, just part of the cycle of being there, so we drifted out a freeline and slipped our snapper rods in their holders, letting the lines dangle, and leaned back for our first morning beers and cigarettes.

The early breeze had dropped off, and the sea was as flat as a sheet of lead. Hot already. Hot and still. And it not even nine o'clock. There was one bitch of a sun coming on. But that's what we had laid in two cases of beer for. We knew it was coming.

Sam shook his head, removed his cap, and ran a weathered hand through his hair. He flicked his cigarette butt over the stern.

"I wonder if it's any hotter off the East Coast or off Florida."

"Probably. August's the same everywhere I've ever been, but I've never been out of the South. More breezes some places. Still hot as hell."

I could see the Standard Oil refinery at Pascagoula in the pass between Petit Bois and Horn. A haze of smoke hovered right above the plant, the burn-off torches holding steady and straight up like lit dark candles sticking out of the sea.

Back in the old days, before he could afford a Loran to feed coordinates into, Sam would run a course out to the general vicinity of the wreck, then jockey the boat until the main stack at Standard just touched one side of his upheld thumb and the western-most marker on Petit Bois touched the other, then he'd run north and south until the depth-finder indicated the wreck. We trusted his thumb in those days.

Sam belched and leaned and tapped his rod with his beer can.

"Guess we ought to reel in and put on fresh bait. My rod's jiggled a few times. Goddamned trigger fish, I bet."

I nodded and threw away my cigarette and reeled in too. The bait was gone, so we both strung on cigar minnows and dropped the heavy lead weights back down until they bumped the bottom, then set the drag and holstered the rods and waited.

The morning wore on, the furnace of the sun building and building until we were drenched with sweat and downing one beer after another. Funny, but you can drink a six-pack in thirty minutes out there in the sun and not feel much more than a mild buzz—the heat sweats it right out of you, what you don't piss away.

We picked up a snapper each an hour or so apart and Sam landed a small grouper, but we had to wait, as we always did, for the feeding hour, which would come whenever the fish were ready, the hell with us and our bait, and when it came we would fill the box. It always happened—if we had the time and patience. Sometimes it would be on up in the morning, sometimes early afternoon, sometimes mid-afternoon, but it always came.

There was a time when we got out to the wreck before daylight and caught all we wanted before the sun got fierce, but we got old, or older, and neither one of us liked to get up at three o'clock anymore to make that run in the dark, around logs and crab traps in the river and only God knew what in the Gulf. Then we had to find the wreck in the dark, hell enough in the light of day, and nearly impossible before sunup—but we used to do it, sometimes circling for an hour until we finally saw the depth-finder spike. And if we happened to be looking away or didn't have the light right on it when the needle leapt, it was like not having run over it at all. You couldn't see the boat wake well enough in the dark, even with the light, so that you could just circle back over the same path. We would know by our Loran readings that we were right on top of the damned thing, but you had to be ready with a buoy when the needle spiked or you might as well start over on the circle again. It's just a hell of a lot harder in the dark, even when you know you're just as close to it as you would be in the daylight.

Like I say, we got old. So we stopped that early foolishness. We weren't kids anymore and didn't have the patience to flounder around in the dark. What's the fun of coming out if you catch all you want before the sun's up and have to go right back home without getting to smoke cigarettes and drink all that beer? So what if you miss that early feeding period—you just wait for the next one.

That's what we were doing, waiting for the next dinner bell, which usually announced itself with both our reels screaming out and the rods groaning and arching almost to the water, the lines singing. And, by God, you can't do more *than* wait. The schedule down there doesn't take you into account at all, not at all, your boat and you no more to the laws that operate beneath that water than a log migrating with the Gulf Stream. If you have your bait down there when the fish feed, they will take it, and if they are *really* into feeding they will snatch just about anything you drop to them—mackerel strips, squid, croakers, cigar minnows, or a piece of tennis shoe, if it smells bad enough. So you wait.

It happened just as we were finishing our sandwiches and eighth or ninth beer on up around noon, just like the fish decided to join in our lunch hour. The sun, straight overhead, was hammering down, the sea was dead flat, slick as oil, the anchor line slack, not much more movement to the boat than we would have had on a slab of stone. Then the reels squawked, simultaneously, as if on cue, and Sam's half-can of beer hit the floor in a gush of foam as he lunged for the rod.

On his knees at the gunwale, he leaned back against the heavy downward pull as I stood solidly planted against whatever was trying to pull me down. We cranked as we lowered the rods a couple of feet or so, pulled hard, then cranked again, winching the fish up a coupla feet at a time until with one smooth motion I swung mine into the boat, just behind Sam, and he swung his in just behind me. Two fine snapper, at least a dozen pounds each, like twins. Brief fumbling with the hooks and we scooped the fish into the box with the others, baited, and dropped the weights again.

For half an hour we baited, dropped the lines, hooked, boated the fish, baited and dropped and hooked and boated again until our arms ached. There was no time for beer or a cigarette, no time for anything but breath and muscle as the fish tried to pull us down and we tried to pull them up.

"God, I love this," I heard Sam say, time after time.

"I need to piss, I've got to piss," he said once, but he went on fishing. Pissing could wait. Beer and cigarettes could wait. This was what we had come for. This was snapper fishing.

Then, quite abruptly, it stopped. No strikes. No jiggling of the line. The rods went dead, the lines tight from their weights alone. Not even nibblers.

"What in the hell is happening here?" Sam had holstered his rod and was unzipping. He peed into the sea. "Man, this ain't right."

"I don't know. Shark maybe?"

When the feeding period ends, it doesn't end abruptly like that. It slacks off gradually. You are dropping the line and catching a fish every time, a process that usually takes three or four minutes, depending on how long you have to fight him. Then the big fish begin to fill up and lose interest and the nibblers set in on your bait and you catch a decent fish every second or third drop, then every fourth or fifth, and on and on until finally you conclude that lunchtime is over and you have to decide whether to wait for the next feeding or go on home.

"There's something down there." Sam was leaning on the gunwale and squinting into the water. "A shark or something has run the snapper and ever Goddamn thing else off the wreck. Ain't nothing even nibblin'." He lit a cigarette. "God-damn, that was going good."

I nodded and opened the fish box. "Hell, Sam, we got at least twenty or thirty good fish in here. It's not like it's been a bad trip."

He popped open a beer and tilted it back. "Yeah, but it quit too damned soon. Something ain't right." He leaned and looked back into the water.

I leaned and looked too, my shadow weaving slowly beside the boat like some dark dancer. I expected to see nothing but sea, deep greenish blue sea. But there was more, something black and enormous, darker than my shadow, one of the strangest shapes I've ever seen, more like a wing stretched to filament thinness, but before I could utter a sound Sam's voice came to me, a sharp, distant whisper.

"Christ, look at that!"

I wanted to raise my head and look, but I couldn't tear away from what I was seeing on my side. "What in hell, Sam, what in hell is this over here? Look here." I gestured to him without turning my eyes from the thing below me.

"I don't know what you're seeing, but over here is one of the Goddamn biggest devilfish I've ever seen, and I ain't seein' but a part of him. You see him from that side too?" His voice was thin and squeaky, the way it used to get when we were kids together and talked about girls we wanted to take the clothes off of. Kind of goofy, silly, almost shrill.

"I don't know what it is over here, but I'm not seeing but part of it either."

I could feel the boat shift as he left his side and slid up to me, thrusting his head out over the water.

"Oh, shit, it's the same fish, man, a giant manta ray, a damn devilfish." He turned and looked at me. "That sonofabitch is at least eighteen feet wide. He's stickin' out on both sides. Just slid right up under the boat. Goddamn!"

I didn't sense any fear in his voice, but his face was a lot paler than it should have been, and he looked a hell of a lot older than fifty.

"What the hell's he doing here, Sam? I've never seen anything out here this big."

The enormous ray just hung there, a few feet down, his wings waving gently like a bird drifting in easy wind.

"I've seen'm before, a couple of times this big, but it don't happen often."

He had fished the Gulf a lot more than me, had worked the shrimp boats and barges, and what he didn't know about it I probably didn't need to know.

"He's just hidin' under the boat, like a damned ling, just like we was a log or something. Restin' maybe, or lookin' for food, the way ling do around the buoys."

I leaned over and reeled in my line. "Get your line in, Sam, or he'll snap it off when he moves out."

I brought in the free-line and stowed the two rods. Sam wound his in slowly.

"That explains why the snapper quit," he said and slid his rod into the cabin. "He run ever damn fish off that wreck when he come up under us."

He handed me a beer, opened one for himself. "They probably won't start up again either. No tellin' what they thought when he come over. Probably thought it was getting' dark already, the way he must of blotted out the sun."

We leaned over and watched his slowly swaying wings. Fish zipped all along his body.

"Them's pilot fish runnin' with him. They got suckers like shoe soles on their heads that let'm attach to him."

"They look like ling," I said.

"Well, they ain't. You can catch the damn things—snag'm with a treble hook—but they ain't fit to eat."

There were jags of shadow wing stretching out on either side of the boat, like a giant open hand curling up to take us in a fist. Sam sat on one gunwale leaning back and watching the wings weave. I sat on the other.

He coughed and leaned toward me, speaking quietly. "I seen one of these sonsabitches hung up one day, not long after I got down here. Some guy had been fishin' out by the old Liberty ships and the ray come up under him, and he just quit fishin' and rigged up a harpoon he had on board—people don't carry harpoons much anymore—and throwed it right through the body of that bastard. Fought him for hours, but he finally drowned him or bled him to death and brought him back."

He shook his head in reverence.

"Better'n draggin' in a shark any day. Anybody can bring in a shark. That thing weighed over a ton and a half, stretched over twenty feet from tip to tip. Half tore his boat up. But he had him hangin'."

He held up his hands and laid one forefinger across the other. "On a cross, like Jesus on the cross, with a spike through his head and at the ends of his wings and one through his tail. Like a big flat, black crucified Jesus. Kids and grownups, newspaper people, everbody come down to see it. Most people didn't have any idea there was things like that in the Gulf."

He leaned and stared at the black wing. "It was like somebody had finally brought in proof of the Devil."

I might have known something was working away in his brain, the way his eyes glassed over when he was talking about seeing that twenty-footer strung up and all the damn people gathered around it, gawking. He pitched his half-smoked cigarette into the water and disappeared into the cabin. I could hear him fumbling around beneath one of the seats, where he kept flares and tools and stuff, grunting and swearing, and finally he crawled out and plunked a giant treble hook, big as ice tongs, at my feet.

"Tie this end to that eye."

He had reached into the rear locker and yanked out the stern line, a fifty- or sixty-foot piece of half-inch nylon cord he kept there. He handed me one end and secured the other to one of the cleats on the transom.

I looked at the piece of line in my hand. "Sam, I don't know what you've got in mind, but—"

He spun around and glared at me. "What I've got in mind is haulin' in my own devilfish and hanging his ass up beside my boat for people to look at and take pictures of. Now tie that line on."

I just held the massive hook in one hand and the line the other. "Sam."

"Then, Goddamnit, I'll tie it. Fuck around all day and he'll be gone." He snatched the line from me and held his hand out for the hook. "Let me have that hook."

I moved the hook away.

"Sam, this is crazy."

"Give me that fuckin' hook!" His eyes were blazing.

I handed it to him. In a flurry of fingers he tied the hook on and the giant treble dangled on a two-foot length of line from his right hand.

"Ain't no way I'm going to let this chance go by. It ain't likely to come again. Not with the sonofabitch that close. Now stand back."

I stood and touched his shoulder.

"Sam, let's don't do this. He's just going to tear up the boat and maybe drown us. If you hook him, something is going to have to give, and I don't think it'll be him."

He turned and glared at me. "I don't expect you to understand this. I just expect you to stand back and let me alone."

He hoisted the hook.

"This is a stainless salvage hook. It ain't barbed, but if you keep the pressure on, it'll hold any Goddamned thing, and I doubt he'll break that line—he'll just drag us until he dies. Did you ever read *The Old Man and the Sea*?"

I stared down at the dark wing on my side of the boat. "Sam, that's not a marlin."

Off to the south two big thundercells were building, leaning toward us.

But I might as well have saved my energy for the fight because Sam stood up on the stern of the boat and held the hook out over the outdrive.

"Get the M-1," he whispered. "If I can get him up close enough, I want you to put a round right through his head, between the eyes."

I scrambled into the cabin and hefted the big rifle from a rod rack. "How the hell," I grunted, "will I be able to see where his eyes are?" Sam always carried the rifle, loaded. I jacked a round into the chamber.

He still stood, watching and waiting, the hook swinging from his right hand.

"He's got little fins that look like horns coming out from the head end. When I hoist the front of him out of the water, just shoot into the solid part between the horns, back about half a foot, and he won't give us much trouble."

"Right." I eased up beside him, the rifle poised. "I think you ought to leave him alone."

"I figure," he said, swinging the hook back and forth at the end of the line, "that I can pitch out just in front of him and come up under, snag him right about where his mouth is. I wish we had something with barbs, but the hook'll hold if I drive it in deep and keep the pressure on."

"Sam," I said, stepping back, "the pressure's already on."

Then he flung the big stainless treble out behind the stern, hesitated, and started hauling the line in, an arm-length at a time, until I saw him jerk tight. I moved way off to the side, to avoid the hook if he happened to yank it back into the boat. Sam was poised against the sky, thrusting with his legs and back against what he had latched onto below. Out of the corner of my right eye I could see lightning break from the base of one of the storms moving toward us.

The rest is just bits and pieces, a sort of stop-frame horror movie. The fish could have sounded and snatched Sam from the transom and into the sea—this I know—and probably taken off the transom too, if the cleat held, but he rose, like some magnificent dark angel, rose until I felt him heave the boat by the outdrive, boiling up a great green dome of water, then turning toward us, not twenty feet out, turning and rising until he completely left the sea, the end of one wing blotting out the sun, sailing with his white belly above us. I could see two streaks of red where the hook had torn across just beside his mouth. He landed, half in the boat, half out, springing Sam like a diver over the outdrive, slamming me into the gunnel. The rifle skittered across the deck and into the cabin.

And then he was gone, off toward the southeast. He struck the line of our buoy, yanking the big yellow marker out of sight, but it bobbed up again. Sam hoisted himself onto the outdrive, sputtering and yelling for me to shoot, while far out behind the boat I saw the devilfish rise, swelling a vast dome of water, his wings gently arching like a dark hand waving goodbye.

The Hands of John Merchant

A ny time I'm back over that way—which is not often, since I've come back to Texas—I drive along the beach road and look out over the Gulf toward the islands, which, when the sun is high enough, give off a little glare so that you can tell exactly where they are without actually seeing them. Like an aura, you might say. It's ghostly. And if I let myself, in those brief glimpses before I have to turn my eyes back to the road, it's not so hard to imagine that I see ol' John Merchant reaching a hand up to me from out of that green water, cupping it toward me, with bright red and yellow spices slipping out between his curled fingers like sand, and I can smell the spices so distinctly that my nose burns and my eyes haze over.

So here John Merchant was again, his skillet almost red hot and smoking, spices singing on the air, while just outside the screen door, evening was softening into night.

I was slouched over his kitchen table working on my fifth or sixth beer of the evening and feeling it from head to bladder while he prepared our dinner, redfish we'd caught in the surf at Petit Bois Island the weekend before. The broad fillets and a few odd little nuggets lay on a piece of wax paper at the end of the table, and an assortment of spices trailed out in a long line of jar lids like something for a witch's broth, carefully measured out, mostly reds and blacks, some greens and yellows. It would all be dumped together in a bowl when he was ready to roll the fillets and throw them into that hot skillet, where they'd sizzle and pop until the smoke that rose from them would take John completely, and his feet and hairy legs would drop out of that cloud like some sort of very human god just touching down to earth.

Then his lean, sun-darkened hands would reach out and whisk up the fillets in one run, like a card dealer, and sooner than I could focus on the flurry of fingers, the spices were gone and the skillet shrieked and smoke billowed up until finally I could see him only from the ankles down, just a great cloud with two hairy feet.

I suggested to him more than once that he get a damned vent fan for the kitchen or blacken the fish on the grill outside. There was no reasoning with John.

This was the way it usually went. Most Saturdays we'd get up early and make a run to the islands, spend most of the day thrashing the surf, and come back in and feast. And if we didn't catch anything to eat, we'd just drink beer and get drunk as coots and sprawl out on the floor of his living room or den or wherever and sleep it off—without dinner. It was a point of honor with him, a little less with me. If we didn't catch fish he wouldn't touch a solid thing, just beer or whiskey, and not eat until the next day, but likely as not, I'd wake up during the night hungry enough to eat the linoleum tiles I was stretched out on and crawl to the refrigerator and graze through the bottom shelves—cheese or left-over meat or lettuce or a jar of olives. Hell, it didn't matter as long as it filled the hole in my stomach enough to let me sleep through till dawn, when I knew he'd get up and fix some bacon and toast and eggs.

John wasn't married—*had* been but wasn't when I knew him back then. His wife ran off with somebody very different from him, which was the way he wanted it, he said. If she'd grabbed on to somebody just like him, he would have taken it hard and probably tracked down and killed both of them. It was that honor thing again. The overweight used-car salesman with his gold necklaces and polyester leisure pants over which his belly hung like a double scoop of ice cream spilling over the edge of its cone on a hot summer day was exactly what she needed, he figured, and he could live with the image of her bearing up under him night after night like a terrible smothering dream. It was better imagining that than shooting her, he said, and spending the rest of his life in prison.

He lived in a drab little house at the end of a drab little street in Gautier, Mississippi, about three miles from a trailer I shared with a couple of dogs, which I was fairly confident would never abandon me for a used-car salesman, and even if they did I'd just get two more. Dogs are easier to come by than women and a hell of a lot less expense and trouble to get *and* keep satisfied. And you can have as many as you want and not have to worry about them killing each other in a jealous rage. Don't have to listen to'm bitching or fretting over makeup. All that shit.

We worked at the big shipyard in Pascagoula, in the Electrical Department, pulling cable mostly, since neither one of us had been there long enough to work our way up to anything better. We were academic dropouts from the University of Texas waiting around for some sort of easy life that just never seemed to show up. He'd talked me into coming to Mississippi with him, since he'd grown up there, but there wasn't much light work around. John had tried his hand at reporting at a Coast newspaper for awhile, and I substitute taught in math in area high schools and did some night security work at a mall, but all that was meaningless and didn't pay enough to live on. Not a year after we moved over there he knocked this waitress up and married her and stayed married long enough for their trailer to turn green, which is about a year in this climate. When she left him, me and John had a one-beer discussion about going back to Texas and finishing school. A six-pack or so later we had decided on the shipyard. Next day we bought some rugged clothes and hard-nose boots and went to work.

Weekends, we fished. Seriously. Like it was a religion. If the weather didn't lay us in, we took off on Saturday morning in John's sixteen-footer, the only thing he kept from the marriage, and stayed at the islands all day, sometimes spending the night out there and sleeping on the beach. We ate what we caught. You can catch fish if you know you're going without food if you don't.

This was one of those Saturdays, though, when the weather threatened early, blowing like a sonofabitch from the east with low white clouds trundling along under darker ones, and you don't want to get caught out there in a sixteen-footer in heavy weather. We already had the beer iced down and the rods stowed when John said he reckoned we'd better wait, so we unloaded the ice chest and spent the day lounging around watching baseball on the tube and drinking beer. Now the only thing between us and a hell of a meal of blackened fish was John's magic with the spices and that skillet. There was a big bowl of salad on the table already, but the fish was what mattered. Jesus, what he could do with those spices.

After a few minutes in the thick smoke he dipped down and out of the cloud and said, "They're about done. You wanna eat outside?"

"That, or we're gonna have to eat on the floor, where we can see what we're eating and where there's air."

"Arright, you get that bottle of red wine out of the refrigerator and the salad bowls and a couple of plates and glasses and silverware, and, shit, some napkins—you know what to get—and I'll meet you on the porch."

Half an hour later, high on the earlier beer and half a gallon of cheap red wine, we finished the last of the fish and studied the weather, which seemed to have washed out over the Gulf like a faded flag.

"I guess we should have gone out," John said.

"Yeah, but we'd have missed out on this miracle you've wrought here, Sir John. You dropped down out of that cloud like God Hisself and broke fish with me, enough for the multitudes, and turned beer into wine. You're even better at turning beer into piss."

"For a fact." He sighed and leaned back in his chair. A crusty piece of fillet lay on his plate.

I pointed to the piece of fish. "You gon' finish that?"

"Naw. *You* want to eat it?"

"Nope. Just thought I'd package it up and send it over to Ethiopia for some poor starving sonofabitch." I reached over and speared it with my fork.

"*Unh-hunnnh,*" he said.

Now, John Merchant was one of those folks of few words. He just never talked much. But when he used that *Unh-hunnnh* as a lead-in, something was coming, something big, something significant.

I held the piece of fish on my fork, balanced it between the plate and my mouth. "What? What is it, John?"

"Well, I was just thinking that most folks believe that all you can blacken is redfish or snapper, but fact is, you can blacken almost anything. It's the spices, of course, and the hot skillet. I'll just bet you could season anything that swims or walks or crawls or just lies flat on the highway and fry it like this and you'd like it just the same. Like barbecue. You can barbecue any Goddamned thing in the world and it tastes good. Rat or snake or squid or—hell, like I say, *anything.* That's what barbecue sauce and deep-fat frying is all about. Making even the worst piece of meat you can come up with taste good."

I finished off the piece of fish and picked up the glass of wine and sipped. "You reckon, huh?"

"Well, back at UT there was this wormy little guy—a business major, marketing, I believe, short and stringy and mousy looking—and a bunch of the jocks in a sociology class got to where they picked at him regularly. Just for the pure hell of it, meanness, because he never done anything to'm. Except he made some remark the second week about athletics and athletes being the bane of American society, setting all the wrong role models and stultifying the American mind, establishing a ridiculous value system, and ball clubs paying millions to people with minds like mites. Just off-hand shit like that.

"Hell, they set in on him like bad yard dogs. They'd do things like track in dog shit and step on his foot, you know, high school stuff, put Elmer's glue in his books and paste the pages together, goofy stuff. Whisper, 'Hey, faggot.' Just silly, juvenile stuff, but they really kept on him and didn't let up all semester.

"And he never said a word back, just kept on with his studies. And just to show these ol' boys there were no hard feelings, he invited them to a party at his apartment the afternoon before their final exam. Now, they wouldn't have gone to any party of his, of course, except that there wasn't any way *he* could be a threat to them and, after all, he said he'd have a keg of beer, and then everybody wanted to know how to get there.

"What he did was, he got with a medical-student friend of his and the two of them slipped into the anatomy room one night and pulled out this ol' fat gal that had died of natural causes— or, hell, *un*natural, whatever—and cut a big thick flank steak off each thigh, underneath, where it wouldn't be missed for awhile. Folded the skin back around and tucked it, you know."

"Jesus Christ, John, what kind of shit is this you're—"

"Ol' Gerald sliced up and marinated the meat for a couple of days to take out the taste of any kind of preservative. Barbecued strips of that fat woman's thighs and fed'm to that gaggle of jocks. They shot the beer and wolfed that fat woman and said it was the best meat they'd ever had anywhere, tasty and tender and juicy, and wondered what it was, but he never said a word except that the meat was a rare delicacy, and rare it certainly was.

"News of a mutilated cadaver hit print two days later—they found out sooner than I'd have thought—and the little business major sent a copy of the article and a letter to every one of them football players telling them that he hoped they enjoyed the barbecue. That made them cannibals, you know, which is one of the few things you can't just offhand accuse jocks of being, so all they could do was try to keep it quiet. And they sure as hell wasn't going to bother him, since anybody who'd break in the anatomy room and whack on a cadaver might be dangerous or have dangerous friends. Bet your ass this much, though—I'll bet every time they've had barbecue since that night they been reminded. . . ."

I downed the last of my wine and stared at my plate. "What's your story got to do with this fish?"

"Nothing, nothing, only how do you know what you've just eat?" His eyes were glittering like sun on a sea rod. The wine soothed my burning tongue.

"The only reason you think what you ate was fish is that you saw me get something out of the freezer and take it to the stove," John said. "But you didn't see *what* I got out. I could of throwed anything into them spices and blackened it. It's all in the hands, and in the spices. And you don't have any earthly notion what's in the spices. Might be ground-up frogs or bat wings or dog shit or anything."

I smiled. "I'd know redfish from dog shit, even fried."

"You think I'm kidding." He tilted his glass back, swallowed deep, and looked away at the moon, just coming up over the edge of the Gulf. "There's more things in Heav'n and Earth, Horatio . . ."

"Bullshit, John—"

"You never noticed any difference, did you?"

"Any difference in *what*?"

He was smiling, a secret, dark smile. "Well, I've told you I could blacken anything and it'd taste good. The theory's just been tested."

"Bullshit, John." I stared down at my bread-polished plate. "Just bullshit." I was thinking about a slice of fat-woman's thigh, barbecued and served with beer. "Besides, I never did anything to you."

"Those fat-woman thigh strips didn't hurt the jocks. They enjoyed them and came away kinda liking ol' Gerald, I'd say. Probably the best piece of woman they'll ever get. A good joke's a good joke, even if the one playing it is the only one that knows about it."

The fat moon crept up higher in the sky as I sat leaned back in my chair, smashed on beer and wine, looking over at John. The grin on his face told me he was lying. But who could be sure with John Merchant?

John drowned in the Gulf the very next day during a squall when the last thing I saw of him was his two big hands reaching up out of the tumbling sea toward me while I clung to the side of his small boat, unable to turn loose to extend a hand or throw him a line. The joke was that I never knew he couldn't swim. In all the time I knew him he never told me.

They pulled his body out just inside the cut between Horn and Petit Bois almost a week later, after he'd probably washed way out and come back in with the tide. And I was there. After the Coast Guard picked me up and they checked me out at the hospital, I came right back out and borrowed a boat and helped them search, eating when I had to and sleeping in snatches until on the sixth day someone spotted him riding the currents in the channel.

He was dreadfully bloated and a strange purple and white color, like a blow-up toy that kids punch on, and all kinds of fish had been at him. I wouldn't have known him but for his shirt and pants, and his hands. Everything on him was swollen like a balloon, but his hands—somehow they looked the same,

same color and shape, his fingers curled like they were reaching up for my hands or down to pick up fillets.

I live in Galveston now, but I stay away from the Gulf. I have tried to blacken fish since, but I can never get the spices right. I get close enough, though, and the spices and beer and smoke always take me back to John Merchant and that evening when he may or may not have played a big trick on me. Who could know what thing with wings or fins or scaly legs he had waved his dark hands across and transformed with magic spices and fire and served me with blood-red wine?

Islands, Women, and God

"What is it that you keep looking for out there?" my wife is asking. Or at least that's all I hear of what she's asked.

It is late on a Sunday afternoon in October, and I am standing on the deck of our new house, hands propped on the railing, looking out over the marshlands of the Pascagoula River toward the mouth, where it empties into the Gulf just west of the shipyard, whose cranes are poised like the cocked necks of wading birds among the bright lights emblazoning the crossbraces of long gray ships. Beyond them lie the barrier islands, which at this distance I cannot see. A light wind off the Gulf is riffling over the marsh grass in waves.

She is standing behind me with a drink in each hand. I half turn to her.

"Nothing." I reach for my drink. "It's nothing."

Dark thunderheads lean to the east out beyond Horn. I can see the dappled play of lightning high in them and at their bases an occasional jagged streak.

"It's like you're waiting for something," she says, easing up beside me.

"No, no." I toss my drink in one gulp and take another long look in the direction of the islands. "I'm just thinking about Ray."

"Oh," she says. "Oh."

"See you boys," he said that Friday afternoon in June when he punched out at the shipyard for the last time—only we didn't know that then. We just heard what he said and saw him get in his truck and leave, turning not left toward his house, but right toward the beach and the dock by the Coast Guard station, where his boat was tied.

We were surprised when his wife called a couple of us later that night to ask whether we'd seen him at work, since he'd gone off in his boat like that often enough that it shouldn't have caused her any concern. He was there, we told her, but we didn't know where he got off to, only that he was heading toward the Gulf when he left. Somehow—and I don't have a clue how it works—women always seem to know when something's not right with a man.

And that was that. Twenty-two years at the shipyard and Ray, our foreman and a damned good friend to most of us, was gone. And not just for the weekend, the way he had in the past. His wife called the police early on Saturday, and they found his truck parked down by the dock where he kept his boat, but the boat was gone, along with Ray.

We told her and them that there was nothing to worry about unless he didn't show up late Sunday. It didn't figure that a man in his late forties making a good wage and married to a woman that any of us would have been glad to have—even with a couple of kids still at home with her—would just up and take off in his boat for good.

He didn't show up on Sunday, but an officer from the Coast Guard did—on Ray's front steps. A shrimper had run across the *Prancer* drifting some eight miles south of the islands. When the Coast Guard got out there, they found the boat half sunk and stripped of everything that wasn't screwed down, without fuel. And without Ray. They hauled it in and found traces of blood on one of the seats, but a squall had rinsed the inside of the boat pretty well.

Now, Ray always went out with full tanks, so it didn't make sense that he had run out of gas, and he always kept a shotgun along to deal with pirates, as he called them, the renegade drug runners out there that would seize your boat in a second if they figured they could do it without getting shot. So it was a big mystery to us who knew him well. To the Coast Guard, it was easy enough to figure: Ray'd run into some of those pirates and they had taken his fuel and supplies and given him a nice sea burial by way of thanks.

Fine, we said the next morning in the fabrication shop, if they wanted to believe that, but why would the pirates go to all that trouble for some gas and canned food and his shotgun and fishing stuff and all that and not just go ahead and take the boat? Didn't sound like any pirates we'd ever heard about. And how the hell could anybody get the drop on Ray? It didn't make sense to us, but we didn't have any say in it, so we adjusted to a new foreman and went on with our day-in and day-out lives the way we had before.

It was a Sunday morning in late October of the same year. I had gone out to the islands early with two fishing buddies, Eddie and Mack, who dropped me off on the inside of Horn, pretty close to the eastern tip, to walk across to the outside beach to fish while they went on east to try for trout or redfish in some of the gulleys off Petit Bois. We planned to meet mid-afternoon back where they put me off.

They didn't know it, and I sure as hell wasn't about to tell anybody, but years before, I had found a secluded inside pond on Horn just loaded with redfish and oysters. So I struck out very business-like up through the dunes straight across the island, which lies about eight miles off the Mississippi Coast and runs in a narrow sixteen-mile crescent east and west, at its widest point maybe a mile from inside to outside. The minute I dropped out of sight in the dunes, where the other two couldn't see me, I turned west and headed toward the line of trees that began half a mile or so from the eastern tip. It would be a long haul, but worth it, I figured, since I had rarely come away from the pond without my limit of big reds and my belly full of the fattest oysters you could find anywhere in the Gulf.

In less than an hour I had made the march and settled my tackle box under a palmetto beside the pond, wedging the coffee thermos deep in the sand so that it stood upright and laying alongside it the zip-locks of cheese and crackers and a little jar of sauce to go with my oysters. There was no indication that anyone else had been around the place—marsh grass up to my waist ringed the pond, and nothing looked disturbed except where alligators had slithered in and out in a few spots, their muddy trails criss-crossed with coon tracks, and one set of hog prints came down but didn't leave. An alligator might have taken him, but he probably just worked in the shallows and came out somewhere else. It's a big pond. When I got to the west end, casting all the while and getting only one strike in over an hour, I had to walk out on the higher sand to avoid a boggy place where the water channeled in during rainstorms. So there I was weaving in and out through little clumps of palmetto trying to keep from getting spiked too bad when I realized that I was following somebody else's tracks, moccasin-like tracks, but probably made by well-worn sneakers.

"Now what in hell is going on here?" I asked aloud. I hadn't seen human tracks around that pond more than a couple of dozen of times in the nearly ten years I had known about it, and then they were just passing through. The eastern tip of the island was fished heavily during the summer months, with some camping in the dunes, but folks just didn't generally mess around back in the interior, where alligators lived.

"I'll just be damned."

I laid my rod down and studied the tracks a few minutes, but I didn't learn a whole lot from them, only that whoever had made them had established a pretty good trail for himself over a period of time. He was a small man, I judged by the spacing and size and depth of the tracks, light-weight.

I followed the trail across the boggy mouth of the pond, noticing that every few feet in the marsh grass there was a little pile of oyster shells, and they weren't made by coons.

"Been in my oysters," I said to the wind, which was kicking up quite a bit. It would be a hell of a rough ride back across the bay. "*My* Goddamned oysters."

A man gets territorial, you know, whether he intends to or not. It's just natural. As far as I knew, *I* had discovered that pond. Not that other people hadn't seen it from the air or stumbled across it exploring the island or maybe from just walking from the inside to the outside. And it could be that people fished it and got oysters out of there, and I just didn't know about it. But that's not the same as discovering it and claiming it. That pond was mine.

The way it happened was, it was a day just like this one, only late in August, somewhere in my third or fourth year fishing the islands, and I had come out by myself, landing pretty far west on the inside beach—the wind was laying the surf up too high on the outside and white-capping the bay—and striking out due south toward the outside beach, but the wind was flinging sheets of sand in my face every time I topped a dune, and I kept edging west behind them, determined to get to the outer beach without getting my face sanded flat like the Sphinx.

The short of it is that I cut through a shallow pass in the dunes and stumbled right into the pond before I knew what was happening. One minute I was bent over facing the sandy wind, scraping myself on palmettos and scraggily little bushes, yanking along my tackle box and rod, and the next I was in marsh grass and up to my knees in water.

I waded around a few minutes trying to figure out what I had gotten myself into. The bottom was rough with something that felt an awful lot like oysters, which is exactly what they turned out to be when I crouched and dug one out of the silt.

Well, I just eased out of the water and kneeled with my back
to the wind and pried the crusty shell open, and I swear, lying
in that little pearl boat in its own salty juice was as fat and fine
an oyster as I've ever put in my mouth. I worked it around with
my tongue a few seconds. It was just briney enough, perfect, so
I let it slip down, then laid my stuff under a bush and waded
out and gathered a double handful. I ate two dozen before I was
satisfied.

Once I got around the western end of the pond and had the
wind to my back, just for the hell of it I cast an artificial shrimp
tail out toward the middle and worked it, and, Jesus, before I
had moved it ten feet I had a redfish on that would have gone
a good twenty pounds, if I'd landed him, but I got excited and
laid into him a little hard and snapped the line. Before I was
through I had more redfish strung on than I could carry.

Over the years I slipped in there as often as I could without
drawing attention, ate all the oysters I wanted and caught me a
mess of reds. It was a rare trip when I stayed at the pond more
than an hour. After I'd caught all the fish I wanted, I'd sling the
fish over my shoulder and go on to the outside beach, keeping
well out of sight, tie the stringer of reds to a stump in the water,
and thrash the surf until time to go. Anybody who ever saw my
fish saw me dragging them out of the surf on that stringer or
across the sand from due south.

So you can imagine how pissed I was when I found that trail and
the little piles of oyster shells. I guess it was kinda like Robinson
Crusoe looking down and seeing footprints when he had it
figured that he was the only one on his island. Islands make you
feel like that anyway—possessive, like if you have water on all
four sides of you, the land you're standing on is somehow yours,
and you want to drag out the flag and drive the pole in the sand
and dig in to defend it.

Now, like ol' RC, I had the creepy feeling that someone else
was there and was probably watching me. The tracks had to

be fresh because we'd had a good bit of wind lately, with rain, couldn't have been more than a few hours old. There's always wind out there, so if the rain don't wash out the tracks, the damn wind'll fill'm with dry sand in a little while. But the path they were on had been trampled down pretty hard over a period of time, and it wasn't alligators or coons that did it.

"Damn!" I didn't give a damn who heard me.

I turned toward the thin line of trees that straggled in from the west between me and the inside beach. They were already stripped down for winter and I could see osprey nests clotted like cocoons in their leafless branches. Suddenly they didn't look as friendly as they used to.

"This is ridiculous," I muttered as I walked back toward my tackle box. "Many times as I've been here, I got a higher claim than him."

I kept turning around and looking back toward the western end of the pond, like I was afraid some little brown savage would come at me out of the high grass with a spear.

"What the fu—"

Out of the corner of my eye something seemed wrong about the spot where my tackle box was supposed to be. There was.

"Hey, man. Enjoyed them crackers and cheese. And the coffee. Thanks for thinking about me. I'll just save the sauce for later."

It was Ray, that Goddamned Ray, sprawled back beside the palmetto, grinning, one stringy brown arm propped up on my tackle box, the little jar of sauce in his hand, the other cradling the thermos like a baby.

"Ain't had coffee that good in a while."

He was the color of a saddle, arms and legs and face, and had the makings of a full beard the color of dry sand, and, cool as it was, he didn't have anything on but a brown tee-shirt and some cut-off jeans, ragged and bleached almost white.

"Glad you did."

I settled down on the other side of the tackle box and kept my eyes on him. It wasn't that I didn't know for certain it was Ray.

I just didn't know for certain what the hell he was doing there. He was supposed to be long dead, somewhere at the bottom of the Gulf with chains around his legs.

"I thought I was seeing a ghost at first, only ghosts don't brown up like that." I tapped his arm.

"No ghost."

He took another swig of coffee and handed the thermos to me. I shook my head. I figured the coffee meant more to him than me.

"Everybody thinks you're dead." I kept staring at him. He'd slimmed down to high-school scrawny and looked like a piece of leather.

"The Coast Guard, me, the boys, your wife and kids—"

"You want to pinch me to see?" He laughed and held an arm out to me.

"Naw. Ghosts don't drink coffee. Or eat oysters."

I pointed to the western end of the pond. "I saw your tracks. How long you been working my pond?"

He sat up and belched and finished the coffee. "Found it about a week after I come out here. You sure had it hid well. That sonofabitch is *full* of redfish and oysters. You know that?"

He glanced at me. "Of course you know that. This is where you've been catching them reds all these years, ain't it?"

I nodded. "Where do you stay at?" I looked around like I expected suddenly to see an orange pup tent that I'd overlooked coming in.

He grinned big and twirled his hand in a wide circle around his head.

"Everywhere, anywhere, wherever I decide to. It's a big island. Got little stashes all over, jars of water and stuff, but my base camp is way back toward the western end, where folks never go. Just alligators and hogs. And me. May sleep there tonight, may sleep right here."

He smoothed out the sand beside him the way a woman would smooth a bedspread.

"Ray," I said, kneeling in front of him, "you're supposed to be dead. What're you doin' out here? You gotta tell me about this." It was almost like I had come on Jesus in the wilderness. You've heard about Him all your life and you've got this idea in your head what He looked like and what He thought like, but you know He's dead and has been a very long time and doesn't really have anything to do with what goes on here and now, and then you're just walking along on this island one day and you come face to face with Him and you know He's not dead at all. And all your notions of what He *was* are gone and you're looking at what He *is* and listening to Him like you're stoned. Jesus was a carpenter and Ray ran a fabrication shop at the shipyard, and they both came back from the dead, and in my mind, rattled as I was at the time, that put them in the same boat, so to speak. By God, I was all set to listen to the gospel according to Ray.

The call, as he put it, came to him at his forty-fifth birthday celebration when he was standing on the upper deck of the houseboat the guys from the credit union at the shipyard had their parties on. They had drifted it down the river to the shipyard and tied it up between a couple of destroyers and given Ray a surprise birthday party one Friday afternoon. Everybody in the fab shop quit an hour early and crowded onto the houseboat, where there was enough beer and whiskey to flatten the whole lot of them.

Later, on toward evening, a blind stumbling drunk Ray climbed to the upper deck while everybody else was busy at poker and heavy drinking and was looking out toward the islands when a big finger dropped down out of a dark cloud and motioned him out to the Gulf.

Now, Ray had spent nearly every weekend of his life from junior high on out at the islands anyway, fishing or boating or camping, so it seemed reasonable to him that sooner or later the call would come and he would have to choose between his family, which he loved, and the islands, which he loved more. His trips out there had gotten longer and longer in recent years—sometimes he would leave on Friday afternoon after work and not come back until he tied his boat up late Sunday. His wife took it in stride, like she had any choice in the matter, long as she wanted to stay married to Ray.

"It was a big finger, I swear, that dropped right down out of a cloud and motioned me out here."

He was lying on his back in the sand looking at the fluffy clouds that rode in from the south.

"It was probably a waterspout. I mean, Goddamn, man, you were drunk out of your mind. I was there. You couldn't hardly walk."

"Maybe, but it was motioning for me." He fanned his brown legs out and in, making half a sand angel. "And I came."

The Friday he disappeared he took the *Prancer* around to the outside beach after dark and stripped her down and aimed her south without lights to circle until she ran out of fuel. Ray even went to the trouble of nicking himself with a fillet knife and dribbling blood all over the seats, but the rain washed most of it away.

"This is some heavy shit, Ray. I don't know whether Martha has collected insurance yet, but you know she will. That'll make it a crime . . ."

"Only if they find out I'm alive. Besides, Martha never had anything to do with it. And I ain't committed no crime. I ain't took none of the money, if she did get any. She thinks I'm dead too. And you better not tell anybody. I'll trust you on that one. Don't tell nobody."

"I won't. I promise. I ain't got *shit* in this game. I still don't understand—"

"And you won't," he shot back, dropping his smile for the first time. "You can't. If it ain't happened to you, if the call ain't come, there's no way you *can* understand." He grinned again.

"It was like a religious calling, like God was calling me out here to be with Him, to get away from all that crap back there."

"Ray, Martha's a good woman, and the kids . . ."

"I told you, you make a choice. I made mine. I give up on that old life. Maybe it wasn't all that bad, but it come to where it didn't satisfy me, like something was missing."

He'd drawn himself up into a sitting position, his arms wrapped around those skinny brown thighs and shins and his hands clasped together.

"You wouldn't believe—"

"Ray, you never said anything to any of us about believing in God."

"I don't believe in all that church shit, naw. You probably don't believe it yourself. Y'all don't know God at all, just that gibberish about father and son and holy ghost and a crucified man that come down to take our burdens up for us and forgive us and then just disappeared, run off and left things in a bigger mess than ever. You ever see an animal beg you to pick up his burden or ask you to forgive him for anything he ever did? Hell no. That ain't the way it works in the real world. He don't pray and he don't give thanks. He don't give a shit about school or lawyers or psychiatrists or *God*."

He lay back and shoved my tackle box out from him, then made the top half of the sand angel.

"Don't even need toilet paper."

He stopped the motion of his hands and lay flat, spreading his arms and legs like he was nailed to the sand, crucified. "Man, *this* is God."

I just sat there looking at him, not sure at first exactly what he was referring to, but his eyes were fixed straight up, his palms spread to the sky, and suddenly I knew what he was saying.

I just nodded. What else could I do? This guy wasn't exactly the hippie type. Just a conservative good old boy. He didn't go to Vietnam, but he would have if they'd called him, and he never got involved in all the flower-child shit, never wore his hair real long, never carried a protest sign. He just went on working in the shipyard while that stuff was going on over there, making ships that got involved in one way or another in killing people. He *woulda* gone. I know it. And he wasn't into dope.

"Ray, I don't see how you could just leave Martha and the kids, your job and all."

He rolled over on an elbow and propped his head in his hand. "Look at me." I looked. "What do you see?"

I struggled with that one.

"I don't know, Ray, I—"

It was like what I was looking at wasn't Ray at all, just some dark, shriveled reflection of the man I'd known, a brown stem with a head blossoming at the top just like a clump of sea oats.

"You see a man that's about to get old. I am almost fifty years old, and I've never done a Goddamned thing in my life that felt right. At least not till I came out here."

He sat up and swept his arm in a broad arc.

"This feels *right*! I am one with the man in the wind and the west moon."

I shook my head. "What the hell does *that* mean?"

"Sorry. I've got books out here too. I *read*, man, I *read*— novels, philosophy, poetry, all that stuff that they packaged for us back in school and tried to make us read because they wanted us to think a certain way. I never read a Goddamn thing back then. Now that I don't *have* to, I *want* to."

His grin was a mile wide, his eyes crinkled in brown leather folds, and he held his arms out like a shaman.

"That was Dylan Thomas."

"Ray. . . ."

I rose to my knees and looked straight at him, but I didn't know what to say, so I just dropped back on my butt and listened.

His wife, he said, was as good a woman as a man could want, and his kids were wonderfully bright and beautiful, but he'd had the call and all that didn't matter any more. Not her, not them, not anything back there.

He fell into the outline of his angel and smiled up at me.

"I guess I miss her most of all nights when I lie on the sand looking up at the stars and thinking about how completely I could love her out here. Without the kids and without all the complications that go along with having a job and a house and property and cars. If I could just have her one night out here, with this sand and water and that starry sky above us, man, she would never go back there."

"Did you ever ask her?"

"Come on, Roger. Women won't do it. They won't follow the call. They don't have to. They got a different *kind* of calling. They're happy with the house and cars and schools and all, if that's what they figure they're *supposed* to have. Or a damn trailer house parked off in the woods or at the edge of a field that won't grow nothing and belongs to somebody else. Anywhere at all's fine with them, long as they haven't had something better. Did you ever notice that women don't move into a home—the home moves in with them. It ain't a home till they get there. They *are* home.

"If it had been up to the women, this country wouldn't have gone west of the Mississippi. It's a wonder they even came over here to this country at all. Women are just different. If we had started with this, then she'd be fine. It'd be all she'd ask for.

"This ain't Martha's world, and I would never be able to make her fit in. One night out here with them mosquitoes and gnats and sandfleas, and she'd *swim* back across that Sound.

"But I have sailed the seas, Roger, I have sailed the Goddamned seas and here am I, moving the stars that are me."

I didn't know how to respond to that one, so I just sat there listening.

"Yeats and Jeffers," he said quietly. "Poets again, which you don't know about. It was always in me. I always liked that stuff, but I couldn't tell anybody. I guess what it took was age, for the piss and vinegar to settle into wine, you know."

He pointed toward the mainland. "No country for old men, no country."

"You writing it too?" I asked.

"No. You don't write it when you live it. Writing poetry is the way you avoid *living* it. It's like a woman you want to write a poem about but can't. If you're really into loving her, you can't for the life of yourself write a poem about her. She *is* a fucking poem—no pun intended. Complete. Rhyme and everything."

He paused, but not long.

"God, I miss women. Their bodies, their—just women. Women and whiskey and fresh fruit. Those are the things I miss most. But canned fruit ain't bad, and I got enough booze out here to have a nip now and again, and—" He curled his right hand and tapped his head with his left index finger. "Women are where you find them at. And I got lots of them up here."

He guffawed, thrusting his ropey brown neck up like a wolf howling.

"Ain't wrote a poem about'm yet," he said, holding out his right hand again. "Must be love."

I laughed at that.

Then he got serious.

"About women. I'm gon' tell you something else about women, some more gospel, long's I got your attention. Women are a hell of a lot closer to the center of things than men are or ever were or will be. They're closer to the Godhead. They are Nature. Like this island. Man, they got dark currents in them, deeper than ours run, and their bodies and minds are a great mystery. They are in tune with the moon and the seasons, with the motion of the universe. Men are just dreams—or worse, just half dreams, but women are *real*. Men look for the reasons, but women *are* the Reason.

"Did you ever get to thinking about how totally dispensable men are? If we blew ourselves up—and men would be the ones to do it because women create and men destroy—and there wasn't but one guy and a thousand women left, civilization would have a pretty good start, but one woman and a thousand men equals nothing for a long Goddamn time. One pecker and a set of balls to go with it is all they need to get it going again."

He sighed deeply. "God, I love women."

"Then why—"

"Because I got the call, I told you."

After the *call*, he'd stashed goods for two or three years way back toward the western end of the island where nobody ever went, storing food and water in rocket tubes and six-inch PVC pipes, sealed and screw-capped on the ends. He had so many spots that he had made a big scroll out of a sheet of stainless steel he had taken from the shop, scratching in trails and shore boundaries, trees and ponds, and making X's where he had stuff buried, from Spam to water to fishing lures. Every trip out he'd take a load, all he could manage without attracting Martha's attention, and now the whole island was like a shopping mall and he just went to the store that had what he wanted and dug up the stash.

"Hey, let's go get some oysters," he suggested.

So we got up and waded out into the pond and gathered a big double handful each, clacking them down in a pile beside the tackle box. From his belt dangled a sheath knife, which he used to open them, as expertly as I have ever seen oysters sprung. I swear, in less than a minute the top of my tackle box was lined with halfshells of fine oysters. He opened the little jar of sauce and filled one of the empty halves with it.

He nodded toward the spread. "You're my guest. You first."

"My oysters," I mumbled and reached for a halfshell.

Then we ate. His lean fingers zipped in like a diving bird, seized an oyster, swiped it through the sauce, then popped it into his mouth. All the while he grinned and sighed with pleasure, like he was making love. And maybe he was.

After our lunch of oysters and water from a little glass bottle he had hidden in a clump of grass, he answered some of the questions I pressed on him. How'd he get fruit and other supplies he needed? From shrimp boats mostly, anchored on the inside of Petit Bois. Sometimes they'd quit trawling along about two or three o'clock in the morning and pull in for the crews to sleep for a few hours, and he'd swim out to the channel markers and just hang around until the lights went down and everything stilled, then ease over and climb aboard and find the galley and take whatever he needed.

"Nobody ever caught you?"

"Been pissed on once by somebody in white rubber boots that come on deck as I was getting ready to scale the side. I just flattened next to the hull and got splattered good. No big deal. I dipped down and washed off and give him time to stumble back to his bunk and went on and got what I wanted. And I got seen just one time, that I know of.

"I was on the way out with a sack of oranges under one arm and a sack of roasting ears under the other when this sonofabitch, cook maybe, raised up from his bunk, which was on the side of the hallway that led to the galley. He just set there, with the moon slanting in on me, bright as day, looked a few seconds, then shook his head and leaned over and picked up his bottle, EverClear or something, and looked at it, shook his head again, and laid back down. I walked on out and slid over the side with my groceries."

When he was shopping, he always carried a small raft out with him, an inner-tube with netting stretched across the center, and loaded it up and tugged it back over to Horn. Just like going out for groceries, he said. And he tried never to take so much that they'd be likely to miss it. With everybody drunk most of the time on those anchored shrimpers, he figured they didn't keep very close tabs on what they ate anyway, just went and bought more when they ran out.

He kept out of sight during the daylight, staying well to the west in the wild interior, where no one was likely to venture. When he fished the surf and inland ponds, he just did it at night.

"People see me at a distance sometimes, but that's no big deal, since they probably just figure I've got a boat on one beach or the other. The only reason I came out today was because I ain't had anybody to talk to in so long—when I spotted you hop out of that boat, I was pretty sure who it was. Started to jump you in the dunes just for the hell of it, but I was afraid you might have a heart attack."

I filled him in on the boys at the shipyard and told him about the kids and Martha. We laughed like old buddies cracking jokes, until he grew serious, the smiling stopped.

"Man, there are times out here, especially at night, when I can get around without people seeing me, that I feel the way old Jeffers must have felt looking out at that eyeball of the Pacific off Carmel. 'What it watches,' he wrote, 'is not our wars.' What it watches, what all this Goddamned beautiful water watches, is *nothing*." He almost hissed the word, the way an evangelist might have said it.

"It just looks off into space, toward where the stars are, and it sees them even when we can't. Great big old sad eyeballs of the earth staring off into space at nothing at all, like they want to go home but don't know where home is. It's the same kind of look I've seen in women's eyes sometimes when the kids or their man's getting to them and housework and—like they're looking through it."

He caught his breath and continued, "Listen, what you see here is God, all the God there is. This island and water and the creatures that depend on it. If they're able to find food, then it was meant for them to find it. And if they can't find it, they wasn't meant to and they die. They work for it, but it's always there if it was meant to be, and nature fixes it so that they always work just hard enough to find it. They're in harmony, man.

"They suffer the same kinds of losses we do. I've seen momma ducks lose half their flock to an alligator and swim right on like nothing had happened, have more ducks later in the year, just like they figured, 'Hey, this is the way it's supposed to be—we eat, he eats, and we get eat.' The ducks eat fish, but I don't see momma fish running around fretting about it and trying to pass laws about them Goddamn lawless ducks. Thing is, out here there ain't but one law, the only law there is. Or ought to be. It's the cycle, man, the chain, and now I'm a real part of it. You ever read that James Dickey poem 'Heaven of Animals'?"

Then he regretted asking. I could tell.

"Well, it's about how all these animals go to heaven and pick up the roles they had on earth: The big cats crawl up onto limbs and wait for the deer to walk under them, and the deer know that they're there, but they go on and walk under there anyway and get pounced on and eaten, because that's what they're supposed to do, that's what nature made them to do. And they're happy about it and so are the cats. It's all being part of the cycle, you know."

When you see this kind of thing in a man, you usually figure he's just a holdover from the sixties or onto something chemical. Ray wasn't either, so I sat right there in the sand beside him and knew that here was the closest thing to real truth that I was likely to ever encounter again, so I just kept my mouth shut and let him ramble, get it all said, all that he had to say.

"I'm in harmony, man, with this Goddamn island, with this Gulf. I got everything I need out here to live, and everything's in balance. Jeffers had the Pacific and granite cliffs and redwoods, and I got this island and the Gulf. I ain't got to run off to Montana or North Dakota to get away from people and find myself, find God. If they don't know I'm here, then I'm not, and it's good as being alone. I'm not a man anymore, Roger—better, I'm an animal. Or I'm getting there. I'm what I was before I *became* a man.

"Every sense of mine is as sharp as a coon's or an alligator's. I smelled you long before I heard or saw you this morning. Hell, I sensed you before I smelled you. The way the animals do. I've been training myself to do without glasses, and, by God, I've just about got to the point where I can *read* without'm, which I ain't been able to do in thirty years. And we're talking about what's happened in just a few months. In a year, hell, I'll be one of them. Nature will take care of you, if you'll let her. I got everything I need right here.

"What but the wolf's tooth whittled so fine the fleet limbs of the antelope? What but fear winged the birds?"

He was up and dancing about now, his arms flailing. "Survival is all, is everything. Back to basics! Back to basics!"

"Maybe so, but all of what you've been eating didn't come from the island or the Gulf. All that canned stuff."

He threw out his hands in exasperation. "Well, Goddamn, it takes a little while to adjust."

"Ray, in a year you'll be dead, the way you've been losing weight."

"All I lost was what I didn't need. What's left is *muscle*." He drew his wiry right arm up into a knotty *V*. "All *muscle*. I could swim to the beach over there at Pascagoula without winding."

I shrugged. "What'll you do when your time comes? When you get old and sick?"

He sat down close beside me and spoke quietly.

"Jeffers has got a poem about a place off in the mountains he stumbled across where all the deer went to die, them wounded by hunters and them that was just old and ready to pass on. They congregated there and died by a peaceful little pool in a ravine. Antlers and bones was all there was left, just antlers and bones, and he says that he wishes his bones was with theirs. And in another he's laying on the side of a hill when a buzzard flies by and checks him out and he says that he was sorry to have to disappoint the bird, that it would be an honor, an *honor*, to be eaten by him. 'What a sublime end of one's body, what an enskyment,' he says. What an enskyment! Whooo, what a way with words."

He got up off the sand and walked halfway up the nearest dune and pointed toward the blue water of the outside beach.

"Roger, my man, when my time comes—and it ain't far off, because nature never intended for a man to get old and helpless—I'm going to dig out a gallon of white wine I got stashed and set right up here on one of these dunes and get blind drunk under a full moon, so drunk I'll have to drag myself down there to that water like a dying deer, and I'm going to strike off south, hard as I can swim, and I'm going to go until I can't."

He hesitated and turned toward me.

"Animals don't have wine," I pointed out.

"Animals don't have anything to forget," he said, continuing: "Then I'm going to get me the biggest eyeful of that moon and starry sky that I can get and go way under and take a big breath of water while I'm staring up, right through the water, at the moon." He raised his face and opened his mouth and sucked in sharply. "Like that. And it'll all go right from there. In a couple of hours my body will be the same temperature as the water's, and I'll be one with the wind and the water and the sky. The fish will pick me clean and my bones will roll with the currents until they settle into the sand. And after a season, after a season. . . . 'It had wings, the creature, and flew against the fountain of lightning, fell burnt out of the cloud back to the bottomless water.'"

His eyes were misty. "Jeffers again."

"Jesus, Ray. This is morbid."

"You might be eating a snapper in a restaurant someday and—"

"Shit, Ray, just cut the shit."

After that little exchange we didn't speak for a while. I studied him out of the corner of my eye as he stared out over the Gulf, and it occurred to me suddenly that we were from different worlds, maybe different times. He looked like a little brown savage, and his hair wherever and however it would grow, every ounce of him pure, purposeful nature, the only thing tying us together the little smattering of memory in what he referred to as his brain vault, and that growing less each passing day as the island claimed him.

"Our birth is a sleep and a forgetting," he had said somewhere during all that talk, quoting one of the English poets, and I figured he was well on the way to forgetting all of us back on the mainland, me and the boys and Martha, the kids, his parents, everybody and everything that gave him an identity in the world that he had run from. He looked like he belonged where he was, that dark, slight figure against the backdrop of sand, and the feeling came over me, just like that, that I didn't.

"Ray," I said finally, "I better head back down to the east end. Eddie and Mack'll be along soon looking for me." I held out my hands. "Not a single damned red. They won't believe it. It's been a while since I've been skunked."

"It happens," he said, grinning. "It even happens to me."

We shook hands. There was incredible strength in his clasp.

"If you're ever looking out this way," he said, walking along with me a little way, while we were deep in the dunes, "think about me. And if you see a big dark finger drop down out of a cloud and crook itself . . ."

"A waterspout is what I'd see," I said.

"Maybe. But you'll know when you've got the call. Thing is—" He had stopped. "This is as far's I'll go. Thing is, you might not get the call but once, so keep your eyes open. And when it comes, you got to forget about everything else and head south."

"It won't come for me, Ray. I'm not you."

He shook his head. "Oh, it'll come. It comes for every man." He shook his head again and looked sad. "Every *man*. Only most don't know what they're seeing or feeling, or they don't know what to do about it. I'm telling you, Roger, an old man over there is, as Yeats says, 'a paltry thing, a coat on a stick.' Out here he's more. He's *everything*. He's a skull full of lightning. He's—he's God, or he's soon going to be, because God is all of this." He grinned broadly. "Or maybe he just becomes a *woman*."

He reached and clasped me by my shoulders and shook me until I thought I was going to have to force him off. His eyes were flashing. "Islands, Roger, it's islands. Islands and women and God. That's my Trinity, man, that's all there is. Islands, women, and God."

I pulled away from him and took a couple of more steps in the direction I was going, and when I turned, he was gone. Like a ghost. The wind was whipping sand over the top of the dunes and stinging my face, so I set my tackle down and rubbed my eyes and walked over to where he had been standing. I could see where his feet had been planted, pointed in the direction we were walking in, but there was no indication that he had turned around and gone back. The tracks were just there, feet pointing toward me, like he had come to the end of the trail and something had snatched him up. The sand rolling in from the dunes above was filling up the slight depressions until, even as I stood there, they disappeared. Then I wasn't certain I had ever seen him at all.

The boys ribbed me that day for not catching any reds to go with the dozen good ones they had in the ice chest, but I had little to say. My mind wasn't on my teasing companions or redfish or the gunnel-hammering swells from the southwest. I turned once to scan the inside beach and the rampart of dunes, but nothing looked out of place, nothing moved, so I faced the coast again and watched the lights coming on as day dropped down to night.

I'm the fabrication-shop foreman now. I've moved up in the world, this world of concrete and steel and satellites. Got a new house and new Jeep Cherokee parked in the garage of it. But, frankly, there's something hollow about my life, like I've seen the other side of things, beyond the surface, maybe like eternity.

It's been right at a year since I saw Ray out there, and I haven't seen anything of him since. The weather turned foul that very afternoon and we didn't get back out to the islands until a warm spell settled in in late December, and that day everybody decided to fish the outside beach of Horn, so I didn't manage to sneak over to the pond. I did watch the sand pretty closely, though, and saw no tracks, no sign of Ray. When later in the spring I got back to the pond, the trail had sanded over completely and I saw nothing but animal tracks and the weaving grooves of alligator tails. I never said a word to anybody about Ray, and nobody's ever mentioned seeing some wild man on the island—I don't recall any shrimpers reporting missing bags of oranges and corn and onions either.

Maybe I just dreamed all of it. For months after I saw him I thought about going out to the college and talking to somebody about the poet he kept quoting, that Jeffers guy—or Jefferson, whatever—but it kept slipping to the back of my mind. You know, the way things do.

My wife is standing beside me, silently sipping her Collins. I look at her and ask, "You like it here? The house, I mean?"

"Yes," she says softly. "It's wonderful."

"Would you go back to the trailer? I mean, if something happened and we had to?"

"The trailer?" She stops sipping her drink and squares to face me. "Why would you ask me that?"

"Would you?"

"*I can live anywhere that I have to, I guess.*" She looks back over her shoulder at the expanse of French doors and windows that reflect the just-beginning lights of Moss Point across the marshes of the Pascagoula, sprinkling the panes of glass like stars. "*Wouldn't want to leave this, but I guess I could. Why are you asking me stuff like this?*" She's giving me a look.

"No reason."

I look past her at the storms, three of them, blended as if they're holding hands, their big willowy heads leaning toward the east.

"*You want another drink?*" she asks.

"Yeah, if you don't mind." I hand her my glass.

"Islands, women, and God," I whisper to the rustling marsh grass after she's gone. The storms are nearing the mainland east of the shipyard. I can feel the vibration of their thunder. I wonder if Ray's watching as the lightning works away high in them, like welding flashes through the smoke of the fabrication shop. I wonder whether he is standing out there somewhere with his face to the sky, his skull full of lightning.

Sometimes I feel like going out there and trying to find him, listen to him talk again, but he probably wouldn't want to take the risk of being seen. I might not find anything—no tracks, no stashes in the sand, no empty wine jug high on a dune, no Ray, and I think that'd be harder to bear than not knowing what's happened to him. I like to think he's still there, sprawled out on a dune toward the western end of Horn, watching the same storms I'm watching. Maybe some day, a day like this, with the storms striding across the Gulf, and me standing out here waiting, a sign will come. But I won't go. I know I won't. I don't have the strength. Maybe Ray did it for me.

Mystery in the Surf at Petit Bois

As a shrimp boat, the *Bayou Self* is awfully small, mainly because it's not a shrimp boat at all: just a twenty-five-foot fishing boat that Joe has rigged up with a forty-foot net and winch. Says that when his wife is along, he has two winches. Frankly, she is built to such scale that she could probably hoist more than the actual winch. Just a big woman, I'm saying. And Joe maybe five-five and weighing in wet at 150.

A small shrimp rig works like a big one—it's just smaller. You got a net that you drag behind the boat, with two big trawler boards that spread it out to either side so that it makes a big mouth that scoots along the bottom with a tickler chain that makes the shrimp jump, picking up everything that you run across, including lots of stuff you want and lots of things you don't.

On the way out, the net rides in a big wad on the picking board, which stretches across the stern just behind the engine box and sticks out over the outdrive a couple of feet. The net's tied off on the stern cleats. Joe puts the boat in gear, low throttle, steering wheel lashed, and we ease the net and trawler boards out into the water. After the drag, we pull the net in from both sides of the boat, stash the boards, then swing the winch out to gather the net and hoist the catch over the pickboard. One yank on the knot in the rope at the bottom, and everything dumps and settles out on the board. We rinse the net and put it back in the water and turn to our catch.

We spread the mass with spatulas and hand rakes, like them you use to dig around in a flower bed, separating the shrimp from claw-waving crabs, flopping rays, anything that can pinch or sting, and throwing them into an ice chest to be size-sorted later. Sometimes there are beer cans and lumps of mud, tar balls, an occasional tennis shoe. Condoms—no shit. Dead animals. And fish of every size and kind: little fish, big fish, pretty fish, ugly fish, familiar fish, strange fish. One of the reasons I like taking these trips with Joe is to examine that seething bed of sealife that spreads across the board in a silver slime. He patiently names the ones I ask about, some really odd creatures, then tosses them overboard. If we happen to net a redfish or speckled trout or some other fish worth taking home and putting in the freezer, it goes in a separate ice chest. That's the way it's done.

I asked him one time what the strangest thing was that he'd ever snagged in the net, and he said that he reckoned it was a cormorant that he scooped up.

"Onliest thing I can figger is that he dropped down between the boat and net and dove for a fish and got swept up."

"I didn't know that they dove, like ducks."

"Me neither, but that's the only way I can figger out how he got in the net. Somethin' else I didn't know is how hard they are to deal with when you dump one out on the pickboard. Hell, he might near beat me to death with them wings before I whacked him upside the head with a spatula and knocked him overboard."

"You kill him?"

"Nope. I tried to. He hit the water and righted hisself and took off. Tough sumbitches."

Joe works at the shipyard there at Pascagoula, and I work at a local welding shop, and ever chance we get, we go fishing around Horn and Petit Bois, a coupla islands in the Mississippi Sound, but when shrimping season kicks in, the fishing takes a back seat.

This particular day we'd been running east and west inside Horn and Petit Bois early on a Sunday, before the Goddamn crowd got out there, using the east end of Petit Bois and the west end of Horn as our turning points. Outside them barrier islands the sea is usually too rough to manage a small boat and shrimp net without risking real problems. Fuck it, let the big boys drag out there.

After a couple of thirty-minute runs that yielded just a handful of shrimp and a dozen or so good crabs, Joe decided to drag along inside the very edge of Petit Bois, which is usually hard to do with the grass beds and all them damn pleasure boats around on the weekends, especially in the afternoons, and the occasional shrimper anchored so their crews can rest a few hours. For some reason, we pretty much had it to ourselves. But it *was* Sunday morning—things'd get a lot busier later.

After bogging down in the grass beds a coupla times, things seemed to be going a little better. We managed one decent drag that yielded a triple handful of shrimp and were probably fifteen minutes into a new run and had just finished cleaning off the pickboard when the boat slowed a little and the nose rose a bit. The ropes had eased in toward the wake.

"Whoa," Joe said, "we done got ourselves a big load there, and we ain't halfway thoo the drag."

Normally a drag yields thirty or forty pounds of whatever it has scooped up, and the boat maintains pretty much the same speed the whole time. The ropes stay at roughly the same angle, and the bow stays stable.

Joe slugged the beer he'd been working on and leaned over the stern, studying the ropes. He'd tied off the wheel the way he often did when we had clear running ahead of us.

"I guess we'd better pull it in and see what we done caught. I hope to hell it's a slew of shrimp, but it's prolly just another damn ton of grass."

I was getting pretty excited. I mean, it's the mystery of it I love anyhow, never knowing what you're going to dump on that board.

"What do you figger it is, Joe? We purty much outside the grass beds now."

"No telling, but we're about to find out."

He put the boat out of gear and motioned for me to start hauling in my side of the net.

The minute I braced against the pull, I knew that it was likely we were going to be hauling in a whole washtub load of shrimp. Or something else. . . . I mean, it's pure-dee wonderful not knowing what you've got in that net, just like when you are wading in the surf or fishing over a wreck and something snatches your bait. It ain't like fishing inland, where you got a real good idea from the bait you're using what you've got on and an even better idea about how big it's likely to be.

Out there in that gulf, though, sheeeut, what you've done latched onto might weigh a few ounces or a damn ton, and it can have all kinds of weird-ass shapes. I've never caught one with one eye or none, but I gotta tell you that I've heard tell. . . .

Not many things surprised Joe no more, as many times as he's fished and shrimped out there, but I could tell from his eyes that he loved the mystery too. Sometimes he would get as excited as a boy looking at his first real pussy.

One time we was dragging along inside the islands, and he looked up at the day moon and said to me, "You know, we are damn fools for sending rocketships up there to find shit on the moon when we don't even know what we got out here." He waved the spatula toward that wide stretch of water.

"I mean, shit, you'd figger that by now I've seen everthing there is to see, but there's always something different down there, something you ain't seen before."

This wasn't what you'd call a high-yield day, though after a couple of drags we had enough shrimp and crabs for a good meal and two small speckled trout. On a good day Joe could bring in thirty or forty pounds of shrimp and a few dozen crabs, maybe an edible fish or two.

We mostly fished and shrimped on the weekends, so it wasn't often that we had the Sound to ourselves. The commercial shrimpers were usually all over the place, sonsabitches, and your chances of dragging in a virgin area were slim to none. At least they could make their runs outside the islands, which we didn't dare do in a twenty-five-footer. The boat could handle the waves and swells, but wrestling with a net in the outside seas could get tricky. So we stuck to the Sound.

Joe had tried shrimping by hisself a few times, but he said that it was just too hard to do, so he always had somebody with him, usually me or his wife, Clarabelle, who could handle the nets better than he could. They fought all the Goddamn time, so I figgered that one day he'd piss her off to the point that she'd throw his ass overboard, which she could do with one arm tied between her legs.

Like I say, this was big-time excitement for me, since the reason I love going out with Joe is that you never know what you're gonna dump on that pickboard. I've seen everything from fruit jars to a pair of panties and everything in between, and that was just my third trip out with him. When that net moves over the bottom, it fans out forty feet, stretched by the boards. The tickler chain scoots over the bottom to stir up the shrimp, and the mouth of the net opens like the maw of a monster fish to catch any that decides to jump. Anything you run across is going to get swallowed and shoved to the rear by the water pressure. The bigger load you got, the greater the resistance against the water flowing through the net.

Well, when we started hauling in the net that day, hand over hand, it was clear that we had run through—and caught— something of considerable size, unlike the twenty to fifty pounds of stuff a drag usually scoops up.

"Whaddaya think, Joe?"

"Got no idear, but I'm figgerin' we might ort to get the gaff or rifle, depending on whether we want to bring it in dead or alive."

We were both straining against the pull, one foot on the stern and the other on the deck, and it was all we could do to move the net in close enough to slip the winch hook through the pick-up eye.

"One hell of a fish," Joe grunted. "Or Volkswagen. Or shitload of shrimp. Lord, what a haul!"

Finally we inched the net up to the point to where Joe could hook it on the winch cable. Now all we had to do was crank down on the handle and hoist the catch-basin of the net over the stern and dump our haul onto the pickboard. It was one of those winches you sometimes see in the bed of a pickup, with a three-inch-diameter galvanized arm six or eight-feet long. A woven stainless-steel cable runs through eyes on the bottom of the beam back to a spool that you turn with a handcrank, unless you are rich enough to afford an electric winch—and Joe was not. It was bolted to a plate on the stern.

When he had the hook through the eye, he stood back and started cranking. The net didn't move. The stern started settling deeper in the water.

"Whoa, man, what in the hell is going on here."

He cranked a few more rounds, and slowly the net started rising. The winch was groaning.

"What in the hell have we done caught?" It was like he was asking the dark water itself.

Joe was cranking down as hard as he could on the winch handle, but the net was barely rising out of the water.

"Good Lord," he grunted, "what in the fuck have we done caught?"

Most of the catch-basin of the net was still well underwater, but I could see that there was something really big down there, big and light-colored, and it didn't seem to be moving.

"Looks big as a refrigerator, Joe."

"Feels like one."

He was still cranking away, and the net wasn't coming up, but the stern was easing down.

"I just don't—"

That's all he got out before the plate the winch was mounted on pulled loose, yanking off a big chunk of fiberglass from the stern. He had mounted it to the boat by running four heavy stainless bolts through the mounting plate and the deck of the stern and through a rectangular piece of reinforcing plywood underneath and then a stainless-steel plate. I don't care how good you got something like that bolted down on a boat, if the weakest link is the fiberglass, that's where she's gonna bust. And bust she did. The winch went right off into the water and almost jerked Joe in with it, he was so clamped on that handle.

"Just look at that, Goddamn it." He was in front of the motor box pointing at the big hole in the fiberglass decking at the right end of the pickboard. I could look right down at the outer shell of the stern.

"Just look at what it done to my boat!"

"So what do we do now, Cap'n?"

He leaned way out over the stern and studied the wad of netting that was draped on the outdrive.

"Well, we can't do anything until we get that propeller free. Turn that motor off. If we knocked it in gear, the prop'll tear up that Goddamn net. I gotta jump in and drag it off of it. And you go thowe out the bow anchor. I don't want the boat driftin' back on me until I get that fuckin' net aloose."

"What if that's a shark in the net? I couldn't tell much about it, but it's shernuff big. And if it is a shark, he's gonna be plenty mad."

"Ain't no other way that I can see to do it. Once I get the net free, we can start up and drag it over there near the beach and haul whatever the hell that is in it up on the sand."

He yanked off his shoes and clothes down to his underwear and slid over onto the outdrive and dropped into the water beside it. He looked unnaturally white in that dark water, like something kept out of the sun a long time, which was weird since he was in the sun *most* of the time.

Freeing the net wasn't as easy as he thought it would be. The winch, which normally would have hoisted the net up and swung it over the outdrive and then on up and over the pickboard, had simply dropped it directly onto the outdrive and propeller when it fell, and whatever we'd scooped up was hanging deadweight, with the weight of that damn winch added to it.

After he had fooled around with the mess a few minutes, he hoisted himself onto the outdrive.

"Got that net wedged down on the propeller shaft so tight that I don't see no way to get it off without cuttin' it off, which I hate to do. That net ain't a year old. Cost me a chunk of change too."

The problem was that the boat was in one of the deeper cuts that run out from the island, and the water was over Joe's head, so he didn't have any way to brace against the pull of the hanging net.

"Can you see what we caught?" I asked him as he clung to the outdrive.

"Naw. That water's just too churned up in here."

"No idea?"

"None."

"So what do we do now?"

He pointed toward the beach. "We gotta thowe that bow anchor out and pull our way to shaller water where we can stand up and get some leverage. That way we can save the net and whatever's in it."

So it was agreed—he'd get back onboard, and we'd throw the bow anchor as far toward the beach as we could, set it, then pull the boat a few yards toward the beach, then do it again and again until we were in water we could stand up in.

So there we were, inching the *Bayou Self* closer and closer to the beach by throwing out the bow anchor, setting it in the sand, and then hauling in the line, which was a bitch, even with both of us pulling on it. When the line got short and the anchor tripped, we'd pull it up and sling it out in front again.

After about a dozen casts and pulls, we were close enough to the beach on the inside of Petit Bois for Joe to drop overboard without floating his cap. He was satisfied that the bow anchor was properly set, so he took the stern anchor out of storage and climbed over the side and waded toward the beach.

The stern anchor is a lot smaller than the one in the bow, so it won't set firmly enough for you to do much pulling on it. The plan was to wade up near the beach and just pull on the line until the boat swung around to where he wanted it. The wind was out of the south, laying the boat away from the beach, so we didn't have to worry about it getting grounded, which would have added just another turd to what was turning out to be a real shitty day.

The problem was that the net, with whatever the hell we had in it, was doing its own job of anchoring, so I slid overboard too and the two of us tugged on the stern line until the boat was parallel with the island and as close as we could get it without straining a gut to the point of busting. Then Joe set the anchor the best he could, and we waded out and unhooked the net from the outdrive and, after Joe crawled onboard and unhooked the main lines from the boards and cleats, started dragging it to the beach.

I'm telling you, that was some tall order. The net, when wet, weighs well over a hundred pounds, what with the tickler chain and stainless-steel rings and shit sewed to it, and then there was that unbelievably heavy cargo trapped in the end of it. The winch was all tangled up in it too, which made it just that much heavier.

Finally, though, we had it lugged far enough up the slope to where we could get an idea of what we had caught.

We waded out to the bulging catch bag.

"What *is* that, Joe?"

He leaned over and poked at the mass in the net. Because we'd been dragging so close to the island, we'd picked up a lot of seagrass, and the water was murky from our agitation, so he had to claw around a few seconds until he stood back, hands on his hips.

"It's a pig. A Goddamn hog. A hell of a big hog."

I eased up beside him and looked, and sure enough, there it was: snout, ears, and a huge white body wrapped in seagrass.

"Nothing to do but drag him on up enough that we can work him out of the net. I ain't cuttin' my net up to get that sonofabitch out."

So we yanked the tie loose on the bottom and started trying to fish him out.

I don't know how much it weighed, but we wore ourselves out getting that pig free of the net. The sonofabitch didn't float at all. Totally waterlogged. Finally, using the surf to propel him, we had him enough up on the beach that he stayed. He must have been five feet long and almost two feet across. I'm talking about a big-ass hog.

"How do you rekkin we managed to catch a full-grown pig out here?" Joe was studying some kind of markings on the side of the hog.

"That's a hog, not a pig, Joe, enough to keep a family of four in pork for a full year, and the only answer I can give you is that I have no idea."

"Used to be there was wild hogs out here on the islands, but cholera killed'm off sometime early last century, even killed off the buzzards out here, but wild hogs don't come in this size or color, and I never seen one that had Chinese writing on his side."

"Chinese writing?"

"Yeah, or Korean or Vietnamese or something." He pointed to some small characters along the flank of the hog.

"Yeah, this is flat weird. Can you read it?"

"Naw, fool, I don't know Chinese."

He patted the hog on the side. "You know, he ain't swole up any that I can tell, and the fish ain't been at him except around the ears. Maybe we ort to try to load him up and take him back to barbecue."

"You crazy, or what? No way I'd eat any of that hog."

"I was just jokin' about that, fool. I figger this is at least four or five hundred pounds of wasted pork. What you rekkin we ort to do with him?"

"Launch him. Let the fish eat him."

He studied the side of the hog again. "Man, I wish I could read Chinese. I bet there's something spiritual going on. Got Chinese writing all over him. If he wudn't so damn heavy, we could roll him over and see what's wrote on the other side."

"It ain't worth it, unless you figger you're going to learn Chinese while we're trying to roll him over."

"It's a shame to waste him. That's a fine hog. *Was* a fine hog."

"Joe, I'm beginning to feel strange about this whole thing. I think that we ought to shove that hog back in the water and gather the net and get on home."

He stood back. "Well, I don't intend to burn no more energy on him. Let's leave him here and let the tide ease him out. If he don't go, the buzzards will take care of him."

We wadded the net up and lugged it out to the boat and hoisted it onboard, then laid the winch on top of it and pulled up the anchors and started home. Across the stern, with the big hole gouged out where the winch had been, I kept watching as the hog got slowly smaller, a long white blister in the wash of surf, and wondered whether there was some sort of significance in all of it, what message was written on the side of the hog.

As Joe says, it ain't no end of mysteries when it comes to the sea. You just stand back and see what the net drags in next.

I thought about the hog quite a bit the rest of the day but didn't come to any kind of conclusion about what was going on with it. I wish we had had a camera to take a picture of that message and see what did it say, but we didn't, so that was that.

Late Monday night ol' Joe called me just as I was gettin' ready for bed. My wife was already asleep, but the phone woke her up.

"You seen the story in the papers about our *pig*?" He sounded real agitated.

"Naw, we don't get no paper. What *about* our pig?"

"Meet me down at Denny's in the morning, around eight, and I'll tell you."

"I gotta work, man."

"Me too, but I'm going in late. This'll be worth it. Meet me there, around eight."

"Shit. Arright. I'll be there."

"What's this about a pig?" my wife asked me after I'd hung up. "What you done got into now?"

"I ain't got into nothing. Go your ass to sleep."

So the next morning, bright and early, we were sitting at a table in Denny's drinking coffee and looking over a story that had appeared in the local paper.

Joe tapped the paper. "See what it says right there? Some assholes out there on Petit Bois fished that pig outta the surf late Sunday, and it was stuffed full of dope and wads of hunderd-dollar bills. Might near half a million dollars in it."

"*Our* pig? That pig we netted?"

"Well, they said it had some kind a strange writing on it, so I 'spect it was. I can't imagine that there's that many hogs with writing on'm in the surf on Petit Bois on Sunday afternoon, without you count the fat-ass white trash women and their tattoos."

"Well, how in the hell did they know the money was in the pig?"

"The paper don't say, but I talked to a friend of mine that works for the shurf's department, and what happened was that something—bluefish or shark or barrycuder—ripped him open along the side, and one of them bags of dope, something white, was hanging out. That's when they decided to check it out. They drug him up on the beach the best they could, using the surf to wash him in, the way we done, and cut him on open, and there was all this damn dope and money in ziplock bags."

"How'd they get all that in the pig?"

"Cut him open just enough to get it in there and then sewed him back up. If we had rolled him over, we'd of saw the stitches."

"So we had a damned half-a-million-dollar-plus pig in your net and let it go."

"We didn't exactly let the sonofabitch go, if you remember. . . ."

"Yes, hell, we did. We left him rolling in that Goddamn surf."

"Well, fuck you. It ain't like we had any way to suspect that that hog had anything inside him but—"

"Aw, Joe, I ain't blaming you for nuthin. It's just when I get to thinking about half a million dollars. . . ." What I was thinking about was that sorry-ass trailer I live in and a sorry-ass wife that don't work.

"And all that dope."

"Why didn't the people that found it just keep the dope and money, rekkin? Wouldn't *we* have?"

"The boys down at the shurf's department figgered they just got spooked by the dope. And there was a whole lot of people out there on the island, the way there always is on Sunday afternoons. They couldn't of walked off with anything without somebody seeing'm."

"Joe, what would we of done if we'd cut him open and found all that stuff? Think about it."

He took a deep shot of coffee and grinned.

"No fuckin' thinkin' to it: dump the snoot and keep the loot. Nobody'd ever have knowed about it. But noooo, Goddamn it, we had to leave that half-a-million-dollar hog rollin' in the surf."

"And ain't no tellin' what the dope woulda brought down in New Orleans."

"Aw, naw, man, no way I woulda got into that shit. You can get killed real quick messin' around with that stuff."

"Or takin' money that ain't ours."

"Nobody would have ever found out about that. Cut the pig open, fish out the money, dump the pig and the dope back in the Gulf."

"And what if it was to belong to the Dixie Mafia or somebody like that?"

"The DM don't generally write messages in Chinese," he said. "Or Vietnamese. Hell, I don't know that they can write period."

"Anybody down there at the shurf's office figger out what the message was on the pig?"

"Aw, they had some Chinese and Vietnamese and Koreans look at it, and all of'm said it was just gibberish. Didn't make no sense to any of'm."

"Maybe it wasn't oriental. Maybe Hebrew or something."

"Yeah, or higher glyphics, whatever the fuck that is."

"Joe, they got any theories on why the hog was out there?"

"Yeah. They got it figgered that somebody else was supposed to scoop the hog up. I don't think it was supposed to sink like it did. It was thowed off a ship, and somebody was supposed to come along and fish it out of the water. I mean, they musta figgered that nobody else was gonna scoop up a dead hog. But it got waterlogged and went down, and we are the ones that scooped it up. I think that they forgot about the weight of the dope and cash. Might not seem like much, but it don't take much to sink a hog. All they had to do was leave a little air in them bags."

"I wouldn't know," I said. "I ain't that up on how to float a hog."

"I wouldn't know neither, but I damned sure know what it takes to drag one out of the fuckin' water and how much it's gon' cost me to get that hole in my boat fixed."

I took a long slug of my coffee and asked what else did he know.

"I don't know *nothing* else about it, only that we missed out on the chanch of a lifetime to get rich."

I stirred the now-cool coffee with a finger.

"Or maybe not," he said.

"Meaning what?"

"Where there's one pig, there might could be a whole damn herd."

"A flotilla maybe, huh?"

So there we were, the very next day, loaded up with beer and samwitches and headed out to the Sound with that net wadded up on the deck. Joe had'm put a rush on the winch job, and it was like it had never been broke off, and it was reinforced at the base to where you coulda lifted a damn teenage whale with it. Joe lived up the Pascagoula River, a couple of miles from the Coast, so it usually took us at least half an hour to reach the Sound.

"Goddamn at the traffic," he said right after we pulled out of the dock. "Look at all them boats, and it's a damn *week* day."

We had took the day off. Joe told the people down at the shipyard that he had come down in his back, and I just told the sonofabitch I worked for at the welding shop that I had a doctor's appointment and wasn't coming in. I figgered a good hog hunt was more important.

By the time we got within sight of the Gulf, I could see that it was swarming with boats. There must have been seven or eight in the river with us, all headed south, and for a weekday morning that was plumb unusual. But, Goddamn, there had to have been forty or fifty strung out in the Sound.

It didn't take long to figger it out. Every sonofabitch with a boat in Jackson County was out there dragging for pigs. And by the time we got into the Sound itself, I could see people not just pulling shrimp nets behind little boats but throwing out treble hooks on lines and hauling'm in. There was barely room to maneuver around nets and lines and boats. And, dear God, there was more swearing and threatening and blowing of horns than you'd find on the L.A. Freeway.

It take'n us almost an hour to get past Round Island, which was a bitch of a long way from where we were headed. Joe would slow down, stop, turn, hit the throttle and make a few yards, then slow down and stop again. Finally he just slumped over the wheel and sighed.

The next thing I knew, we were headed back north, and even then the water was so crowded that it took forever to get to the river. I didn't say or ask anything. I already had it figgered out.

Once we were in the river, he headed over into one of the joining lakes and dropped anchor.

"Might's well have some beer, I rekkin," he said. He took the lid off the box and fished out a couple of cans.

"You see what we done?" he finally asked. "There's more boats in that Sound than there would be for the Blessing of the Fleet. Every motherfucker that can get out there with a net or a hook is thrashing the hell out of that water. There won't be a single shrimp left inside them islands, much less a Goddamn hog."

"It's a damn Wednesday. Don't nobody work no more?" But the second I said it, I realized how goofy it sounded.

We set there drinking beer and watched the steady stream of boats headed down the river, everything from full-size shrimp boats to skiffs.

"Word sure got around fast, didn't it?" He was on his third beer by then and wasn't in the best of moods. "And we had our hands on that pig. Had him in the net, had him in the surf. We was within inches of half a million damn dollars and left it in the surf! Goddamn it!"

He hurled his half-finished beer as far as he could throw it, and we headed home.

I've thought about it a whole lot since then, and I still don't know what to make of it all. And neither does Joe. We don't talk about it much. There never was anything else in the paper about the pig and no reports of anybody finding another one.

From time to time we'll sit down and try to sketch out the characters on the side of the hog, but neither of us remembers enough about it. Joe tried to get his law-enforcement buddy to see could he find a picture of it that they took out there on Petit Bois, but no luck there. We even got some books on Chinese and Korean and Japanese to see could we find something that looked right, but nothing seemed to click. Joe thinks that the secret is in the message, but I ain't sure.

After a couple of weeks the traffic in the Sound dropped off to normal and we started going out again on the weekends. It's hard for anything to feel routine, though. Our ears are fine-tuned to any change in the pitch of the engine now, and we are always watching for any change in the attitude of the boat or the position of the net. Neither of us says anything about it, and we don't really want to act like we're doing anything different. In fact, we don't do much talking anymore while we're shrimping. Something's changed. The water seems deeper and darker, and we are a little more anxious on every drag.

The last time we were out, I saw the day moon hanging out over the deep water outside the islands and thought about what Joe'd said that day. All that space up there, and all that water down here. Blue over blue, blue under blue, both of them full of all kinds of messages, and most of them we can't even *begin* to understand.

The Drag Queen *and the Southern Cross*

We'd laid in at the piss-ant Port of Pascagoula to take on supplies but ended up hiring a new hand, since we caught the lazy turd that used to work with us stealing out of the cash drawer that Earl kept in the wheelhouse. We never carried a whole lot of money on the boat, just enough to buy a few groceries or some beer if we ran a little short between hauls, so me and Earl both knew pretty much how much money we had on hand.

The box was made out of sheet steel and mounted right under the control console, and Earl used a regular padlock to keep people out of it, which usually wasn't necessary, since neither me or Earl or Willie, who'd been with us for three seasons, would dare violate each other's trust. I'd been with him for nearly ten years, so I knew he trusted *me*.

This guy Pope, though, joined us at the beginning of the season, and he was a worthless piece of white trash that had done some time up in Parchman for grand-theft auto. I sensed from the get-go that he was trouble, but he worked hard enough until Earl was on shore buying supplies that Saturday morning and Willie walked into the wheelhouse and caught him with the bottom pried off the cash box, him still standing there holding a big ol' screwdriver, and a twenty rolled up and stuck behind his ear like a joint. We didn't know it was a twenty until later, when I counted the money. We ain't figgered out yet what that was all about—probly just being cocky. There wouldn't have been enough proof in the twenty behind the ear, but the sprung bottom and handful of greenbacks told the story loud enough.

"What the fuck'r you doin', man?" Willie asked him.

"Gettin' my share of the cash outta that box, nigger. I need some beer. What's it to you?"

Shooooeee, only a guy as dumb as Pope would say something like that to a black dude the size of Willie, somebody that had been a lineman for Jackson State and pretty well eclipsed the doorway, which before it was over Pope probably wished he had got through before he said it.

Usually a gentle giant, Willie slapped him upside the head first and then put a big ol' fist in his gut. The cash went flying just before Pope did. Willie snatched him up by his hair and belt and lugged him out on deck and threw him over on the dock like a sack of potatoes, which probably would have had more sense than Pope did. Willie let him keep the twenty, which somehow managed to hang on behind his ear through the fight and the toss and the *landing*, and we never saw him again, but it did leave us a man shy . . . and the cash box busted.

Later, we discovered Pope's bag under his bunk, which I guess he didn't think about while he was leaving the boat. You don't have much time to think about that kind of thing when you're sailing from the deck to the dock, propelled by Willie. There wasn't shit in it to speak of, so we just jammed what clothes he'd left hanging on the end of the bunk in the bag and threw it over on the dock too. If he didn't come back and find it right away, he didn't have to worry—there wasn't anything in it worth stealing.

When Earl got back with the groceries and other supplies, we told him what had happened with Pope and asked did he want to go on and run a few days with just us three and see how did it work out, or did he want us to go see could we find somebody to replace him. He wasn't too pleased to lose Pope, sorry as he *was* for busting open the cash box, but he just said fine, go on and troll the damn bars and find somebody to replace him. But he had to be ready to go the next morning. Early.

The *Drag Queen* was a shrimp trawler or dragger, which is where the *drag* come from in the name, and the *queen* part come from a Bogart movie, *The African Queen*, Earl said. She was based in Tampa, though the captain—Earl Hitt's his whole name—worked the entire coast, depending on season dates and concentrations of shrimp. A 65-footer powered by a Cummins diesel, the *Queen* could handle most weather in the Gulf, and with her new refrigeration system and an extra-large backup fuel tank, she could stay out for quite a stretch, depending on the volume of shrimp we were hauling in.

A boat that size could get by easy with a crew of three, but Earl wasn't what you'd call a spring chicken, somewhere between fifty and eighty—it's hard to tell when a man has been shrimping the Gulf for as long as he had—and though he was damn good at the wheel, he wore out fast on the back deck. That's a place for young guys with big muscles and little brains and real short-range dreams, like how to spend a month's wages in one weekend as fast as possible without a Goddamn thing to show for it on Monday morning but maybe a black eye or missing tooth or a case of crabs. They gotta be willing to do whatever needs to be done back there—heading shrimp, managing the rigging, or scrubbing the deck—in all kinds of weather and seas without complaining. Oh, they'll bitch and cuss, like sailors, but most of it is good-natured.

Now, hiring somebody to work on a shrimp boat ain't all that easy because working on a *shrimp boat* ain't all that easy. You spend most of the night dragging for shrimp and sorting the haul between drags, snapping off heads, keeping the rigging straight and in good repair, and making sure the deck is clean enough to work on without slipping or tripping and busting your ass. During the day, unless the shrimp are really running and you make some daylight drags, you might be laid up on the inside of a barrier island to rest a bit, but the maintenance goes on, whether you're dragging or not, and somebody's got to cook and wash dishes and all that shit. There's just always something to do. You might or might not have time to take a shower before you get to crash for a few hours before you're out there dragging again. Hell, I've gone four days without a shower before, but didn't nobody complain—on a shrimp boat you don't notice that kinda thing. I 'spect if somebody shit over the rail and wiped his ass with a stingray, nobody would say a word, except for maybe, "Now, there's a little time and toilet paper saved—how come I didn't think of that?"

We figgered we'd knock around the dock a little while and see could we come across somebody who might know somebody that was looking for a job. It didn't take but half a hour to work that beat, and then we were off to the beer joints to see what we could find. Three hours later we had our man, a guy that had just blew into town hoping to find some kinda work to tide him over until he was supposed to meet up with a Christian band of some kind over in Mobile in a couple of months, and he said he wasn't particular what he ended up doing. We wanted somebody longer term, but there's that beggar/chooser thing. . . .

Willie asked him what kinda instrument he played, and he just laughed and said that he was a vocalist.

"You sing?"

"That's what a vocalist usually does," he said, which I thought was a smart-ass answer, but Willie just give him this strange look.

"You mean, like it's a quartet?"

Then the guy give *Willie* a strange look.

"Naw, not a quartet. It's a regular band with instruments and all, and I sing. It ain't all that unusual these days, you know, if you know anything about gospel music."

"I don't know shit about gospel music," Willie told him.

I put an end to it and said, "You rekkin you can do what we just told you you'd have to be doing on the boat?"

He looked at each of us. "I 'spect so. How hard can it be?"

Willie snorted before I got to it. "*Damn* hard is how hard it can be. You think you're up to it, hunh?"

He took a deep swig of beer and grinned. "If *y'all* can do it, I'm sure I won't have no trouble. I can do anything for two months."

"Yeah, well—"

"Never mind, Willie." Then I said to the guy, "Fine, you're hired."

When we told him he needed to be at the boat by five o'clock the next morning, he almost threw the hook, but didn't, so we all shook on it and headed on back to the dock to tell Earl how we had done.

"What's his Goddamn name?" I asked Willie halfway back.

"Damned if I know. I don't think we even ast him."

"Jesus. We shook hands on a job with a guy we didn't even get the name of."

"Don't need no name. Long's he's got a back and arms and legs and halfway common sense."

"Yeah, and as long as he shows up in the morning."

Well, I wasn't sure about the guy from the beginning. He was big enough, strong enough, for sure, but there was something in his eyes that made me feel like he was not quite right. Sort of spacey looking, you know. And the trouble with those spacey looking people is that too often they see things you don't see. Hell, sometimes they see things *they* don't see.

His name was Jackson, we learned the next morning when he showed up at the *Queen* ten or fifteen minutes before he had to, carrying one of them old-fashioned black metal hump-back lunchboxes with a picture of Jesus on it and a huge thermos bottle.

I leaned and gave him a hand onboard and took him to the wheelhouse to meet Earl, who was plotting out a course for the night's drag off Louisiana, where word was the browns were running pretty thick. He set down his coffee and shook hands with Jackson.

"Durwood? I ain't heard that name in a long time."

"Nossir, it's kinda unusual. I was named after a uncle on my momma's side."

"What the hell did the kids in school call you?"

"Jackson. I liked that a lot better than Durwood."

"What's your middle name?"

"Potts. It's a family name. They never found out about it at school."

"Well, Jackson—I'm guessing you still prefer Jackson to Durwood or Potts—Jim and Willie'll show you the ropes. Y'all gon' be scrubbing down the deck real good first, and then checking them nets for rips. We'll be laying in here for most of the day, but there's plenty of work to keep y'all busy."

"Yessir." He held up his lunchbox and thermos. "Where can I put these at?"

"Same place you put your bag. Jim'll show you your bunk."

I didn't see no bag come on with him, but I didn't say anything.

"Cap'n, I didn't bring no bag with me. What would it have in it?"

Earl looked at me. "Didn't y'all explain to him that we might not be back in for three or four days?"

"Slipped my mind," I said. Willie was already scrubbing the deck and didn't hear any of what we were saying.

"You gon' get mighty tired of living in them same clothes, Jackson, but you can rinch'm out during the day and hang'm up to dry. Just keep your underwear on to where we don't have to see your privates."

Earl motioned to the lunchbox. "You didn't have to bring no food with you. I just brought in the groceries."

"Well, I didn't know how long we'd be out, so I brought some stuff along."

"Like what?" Earl asked him. "I mean, just out of curiosity. . . ."

Jackson smiled. "Well, sir, I'm on the, uh, the Bible diet. It's whole-grain bread and vegetables and nuts, stuff like Jesus ate."

"Well, I tell you what, son, that's gon' be some mighty lean eating out here in the Gulf. You gon' need meat and potatoes and cornbread, fish, shrimp—you'll run out of that stuff there in a day."

"Well, sir, I just didn't know. I can eat that stuff, but it's not my first choice."

"Out here you don't have much of a choice: You eat what I cook up."

"Yessir."

"And sure to God, Jesus eat *fish*. I mean, when He fed that fish to the multitudes, you know damn well he eat some of it Hisself."

He turned to me. "Jim, how Goddamn many *is* a multitude anyhow? A thousand, a million, coupla hundred?"

"Hell, Earl, I don't know."

Jackson raised his hand, like he needed to go to the bathroom or ask a question.

"I wish y'all would not take the Lord's name in vain. It is a sin. A real bad one."

Earl shrugged. "Jim, show him to his God—his bunk—and let him stash his, uh, Bible food—I won't even ask what's in the thermos—and then y'all get out there and give Willie a hand."

Well, I can tell you that I was already having some serious second thoughts about this guy. He could eat whatever he wanted to—nonna my binness—and he could sing vocal in a Christian band until he blew his tonsils out, but when he started in on the way the captain of a shrimp boat cusses, he crossed over a line. And then, when we were taking a break and Earl brought out some baloney sandwiches on deck, he wanted to say grace over'm.

"Over baloney sammitches?" Willie asked him. "I've heard of thanking the Lawd for lotsa things, man, but never no baloney sammitches. Hell, I ain't even gon' thank *Earl* for'm. He ought to be 'pologizing to us for them damn things."

"I don't say grace over nothing," Earl said. "I *earn* my damn food—don't nobody give it to me. Y'all ain't gotta thank me for them baloney sandwiches because y'all *earned*'m. I was brought up in a famly where they said grace at every meal, and I never did get it. It ain't like the Lord come by ever week and dropped off the groceries."

"The Lord may not drop the groceries off," Jackson said, "but He makes everything that we eat, and we owe him thanks for it."

Earl belched. "Fine. You thank the Lord for the baloney, but I guarantee you that if you planning on relying on the Lord for your vittles on this trip, you gon' go powerfully hungry."

Me and Willie laughed at that. Jackson didn't.

"The Lord will provide."

"Naw, shit, the *Lord* ain't providing *nothing* out there. He may of put the shrimp out there, and the fish, but you can bet your ass that they ain't gon' just jump up here on the deck. We gotta fill a damn boat with diesel fuel and throw out them damn nets and haul their asses up here and snap the heads off and ice'm down and clean and cook whatever fish we decide."

I put my hand on his shoulder. "Earl, settle the hell down or you're gonna have a stroke and we won't be goin' nowhere. Let him handle whatever he figgers he owes the Lord for and let it go at that." Then in a whisper: "You *know* you can't reason with these people."

He whispered back, "Naw, but thanks to you and Willie, I got to deal with him out there several days."

"It's OK, Earl, it's OK." By that time I had eased him on back into the wheelhouse. "Me and Willie will keep him too busy to bug you about Jesus and his Daddy."

On over in the early afternoon we headed out to the west. It'd take two or three hours to get to where we intended to drag and then set up and actually get nets in the water, and on the way we had to rinse the nets out. We rinsed'm on the way in, of course, but lots of the crap that was caught in'm didn't flush out, and sometimes that second rinse would do the job, especially after some of it had dried out in the sun and wind. You can't leave too much trash in'm or the water resistance will slow'm down. We also did another visual inspection for rips and snags, which we sewed up with nylon string. There's always something to do on a shrimp boat.

This run was planned for three or four days, depending on the yields. Since we were refrigerated, we could stay out a hell of a lot longer, could even head way south for Royal Reds if things looked promising. Fuel cost was the biggest factor in determining how long we trawled and how far we traveled to drop the nets. Earl had extra-large fuel tanks onboard and a big-ass reserve tank so it cost a fortune to fill'm. Generally we spent the first day or two dragging to pay our expenses.

All the while we were messing with the nets, I tried to fill Jackson in on what shrimping was all about. I taught him how the booms and nets worked, what the tickler chains and lines and pulleys were all about, shit like that. Since he would spend most of his time heading, there was a lot I couldn't show him until we got a load on board—then he'd have to watch and learn as we went. Compared to what goes on after a net comes in, everything else is slow motion. Once it's dumped, it's all asses and elbows. Dump that damn net, clean it out the best you can, and get it back dragging. The longer you got them nets out of the water, the longer you ain't catching shrimp. Then you work through the pile, looking for shrimp and fish you want to keep.

So I was explaining all this shit to Jackson while we touched things up on deck, and he give me this real serious look and said, "What exactly *is* a shrimp?"

Well, Jesus Christ Lord God Almighty damn, of all the questions he might of hit me with, that had to of been the strangest.

"You are on a shrimp boat heading out for three or four days of dragging for shrimp that you gon' be taking the heads off of, and you don't know what the fuck a shrimp *is*?"

He frowned. "Not really. It ain't a fish, is it?"

"Naw, it ain't no fish, fool."

"Is it some kind bug? An insect?"

I just looked at him for a few seconds. I figgered he was fucking with me, but you never know about them Jesus types.

"Naw, it ain't no insect."

"Well, you know how they call crawfish mudbugs over in Louisiana. I figger that's just a joke, but—"

"Damn right it's a joke. Crawfish ain't no more bugs than shrimp are, and shrimp damn sure ain't bugs."

"I know you think I'm pulling your leg, Jim, but I seriously do not know what a shrimp is. If sombody come up to me on the street and ask what a shrimp was, I don't think I could tell'm. I know what they look like and taste like, and I know where they live, but I don't know what one is."

"Well, that's the damnedest thing anybody has ever asked me. I'll tell you that."

"So what *is* a shrimp?"

"I am not going to stoop to answering that question. The next time you are on the Internet, Google it and then tell me what you find out. *What is a shrimp?*, my ass. Likely as not, Google will flash something like, 'What planet are you from, fool?'"

I pointed out a corner of the deck and told him to clean it again, that there was still a little slime on it.

"By the way, Durwood," I said to him as I headed off the wheelhouse, "if anybody else ever asks you that dumbass question, just tell him that shrimps are God's spiny little creatures of the briny deep."

Much as I hated myself for what I was about to do, I kinda eased up to where Earl was kicked back with a beer, steering a course west/southwest. When he saw me at the door, he motioned for me to come on in. Which I did.

"How's Jackson working out for you?"

I shrugged. "OK, I guess. He don't know shit about anything having to do with what we hired him to do, but I guess he'll learn."

"Oh, yeah, he'll learn."

He offered me a beer, which I took, then pointed his bottle straight ahead.

"They hauling in some pretty good loads of whites down around the Chandeleurs, so we'll start in just to the south of'm and see what we can pull up."

"Sounds like a plan," I said.

After a few minutes of cruising and sipping beer, I said to him, "Earl, just out of curiosity, if one of your grandkids was to come up to you and ask what was a shrimp, what would you tell him?"

He give me a long, serious look.

"Uh, you mean, like if the three-year-old wanted to know?"

I nodded. "Yeah, uh, a little one like that."

"Well, the first thing I would tell him is that it's a creature that I make my living catching, a creature that made it possible for his daddy go to the junior college for two whole years, that pays the mortgage on the house and the payments on my new truck, that plays a big part in about half the recipes his momma and grandmamma ever fix. That's what I would tell him."

"But what if he pushed, Earl, you know, really wanted to know what to call a shrimp. I mean, what if he was to ask you was it a fish?"

"Then I'd tell him hell no, it ain't no fish. It's a *crustacean.*"

"A crustacean is what I would have told him too," I said.

We rode on awhile, and then I told him I was gonna go check on Jackson and see did he have that corner of the deck cleaned.

When I got back there he was leaning on the rail grinning.

"What's funny?"

"Oh, there's nothing funny. I was just standing here thinking about how wonderful it is to be out here so close to God and the center of creation."

I leaned on the rail beside him. "Yeah, I was thinking the same thing earlier."

After a minute or two I said, "Hey, Jackson, I'm sorry for being a smartass about your question about shrimp."

"Oh, that's OK. There's just so much I don't know."

I turned back toward the wheelhouse and said over my shoulder. "You don't have to go to the trouble of looking it up, Jackson—in case anybody asks you, a shrimp is a crustacean."

"A crustacean. OK, I'll remember that. Thanks."

"Don't mention it. You really needed to know."

I wasn't two strides on the way to the wheelhouse when I heard him say, "But I prefer *God's spiny creatures of the briny deep.*"

"Whatever," I said.

After that bit of goofiness about shrimp that day, ol' Jackson settled in and became what I figgered was the best he was likely to be in the time that we had to put up with him. He was slow at whatever job we put him on, but he did it without bitching a whole lot. Mainly I kept him cleaning up the deck and making sure everything was clear when we dumped our loads. Our nets were 75-footers, and the haul depended on the concentration of shrimp—you might get four hundred pounds, or you might get a couple of bucketfuls. Whether you got 40-foot nets or 100-footers, if the shrimp ain't out there, you don't catch'm, if they are you do. That's simple math. Well, not math exactly, but you know what I'm saying.

And regardless of how many shrimp you swing over and dump, you're gonna get the usual triple load of every kind of shit you can imagine coming off that bottom, fish of every size and shape, cans, tons of plastic, tarballs, seaweed, chunks of waterlogged wood—you name it, and we have caught it or are going to. And all that shit gets dumped right there on deck, where we gotta go through all of it, looking for shrimp. It settles out and covers every square foot with whatever comes outta the bag, complete with gallons and gallons of slime.

Most of the big boats have got big tables with sides on'm to dump the shrimp on, but Earl says you're gonna get crap all over the deck anyhow, so you might as well dump right on it. And it's easier to clean the deck when you're done with a dump—just scoot everything out the drain ports with a water hose and then scrub it down. Don't have to fuck with cleaning a table and the deck too.

You get down on these pick stools and scoot around gathering up shrimp and either heading them and dumping'm into a container or dropping'm in whole, depending on how the captain wants to stash'm. You spend a good bit of your time throwing crap overboard, which means that you or somebody else is probably gonna scoop it up again.

So the cleaner you got the deck when you make the dump, the easier it is to handle everything when it comes. Jackson had already scrubbed the whole thing down twice, once to get it clean, the second time to give him something to do. Now he was mopping it. By the time he was finished, it would be clean enough to eat off of. Not that I ever would. No way.

I went back in to bullshit with Earl, since everything I had to do to prepare for the first drag was done. Willie was through fooling with the nets and straightening out chains and lines, so he came over and joined us.

"Whatcha think, Earl?" I motioned toward Jackson, who was clanging the mop on the rail.

"I guess he'll do. Y'all the ones gotta keep him busy, though." He took a swig of his beer. Then: "One good thing about him is he don't talk much."

"He talks more than you might think," I said.

"Long as I don't hear him, he ain't talking," Earl said. "That's the way I like it. Keep your mouth shut and do your job, and everbody's happy."

"How come I got to be the one that rides herd on him?"

"Because neither one of you knew what a shrimp was."

"That's bullshit," I said. Then I looked at Willie. "So, Willie, what would you say a shrimp is?"

"A shrimp? Well, it ain't a fish, for sure. I'd say it's a crustacean."

"Bastards," I said.

Well, the yield was low the first two nights, so Earl decided to swing back to the east and drag off Mississippi and Alabama and see what was going on. Reports were better from over that way than they were near us or over toward Texas. We had spent the first day at anchorage in Shoalwater Bay inside the Chandeleurs, since if you ain't catching shrimp at night, it ain't likely you're going to do much more than burn diesel and wear out the crew by dragging during the day.

After we had squared away the nets and lines and scrubbed down the deck, Earl fixed us a great big breakfast of eggs and ham and biscuits, with fish roe in grits on the side, and it was fine. Even ol' Jackson seemed to forget about his Jesus diet when Earl handed him a heaping plate. He wolfed it down like he hadn't eat in years. And he probably hadn't had anything like that in a long time.

The second day we headed on back to the east, rinsing our nets and straightening out everything from the night's drag. We didn't have more than five hundred pounds of headed shrimp from two nights of dragging, and that ain't shit for a modern trawler. Earl was bitching most of the way about how much fuel he had burned and how little he had to show for it. Hell, that's shrimping—sometimes it's good, sometimes it's bad, sometimes it's in-between. And it don't matter whether it's good or bad, the Goddamn work goes on.

Jackson did his share, but he was slow at it, and as long as any of us was in earshot, he rattled on about Jesus and God and how wonderful it was to be out there in the middle of the Lord's great ocean, with the birds and fishes and shrimp and all that shit. He didn't know the damn Gulf from the ocean—I guess all saltwater was the same to him.

That morning, before we had breakfast and headed east, I walked out on deck and saw him leaning over the rail just staring at the water and mumbling some kinda shit. Moaning a little. Praying or giving thanks. Whatever. And when he turned around, I could tell he'd been crying. Weird is what it was. And it put me a little on edge.

On up in the day, when we were well underway and the deck was in pretty good shape, I went into the wheelhouse to bullshit with Earl; "That one, Earl, all he does is talk about Jesus. He talked about Jesus to you?"

"Has a whale got a watertight asshole?"

"I figgered. I wonder if he's talked to Willie about—"

"Oh yeah, tried to convert him. Like he's a missionary or something and Willie's a fucking nekkid savage."

"What did Willie say to him."

"Told him he was a Jew."

"A Jew? Why not a Muslim?"

Earl took a long drag on his cigarette, flicked the stub overboard, and smiled. "Because he would try to convert a Muslim. It ain't no converting a Jew."

"You think he bought it?"

"Whether he did or not, he ain't talked to Willie about Jesus again."

"I guess he's turned out all right. He does what he's told."

"You'd figger somebody on Jesus's team would work faster."

"Fersher," I said.

We drug off the Mississippi and Alabama coasts that night, and the pickings weren't much better. Maybe two hundred pounds, headed. Earl was fit to be tied. But, hell, like I say, the work goes on for the deck hands, no matter what. You don't spend as much time separating and heading shrimp, but you got all that by-catch shit to deal with, and the deck's gotta be cleaned off after every drag. Earl could sit there at the wheel and fume about the low yields, but we went right on working.

Wasn't no way he was going to waste fuel dragging during the day with the drags so shitty, so just after daybreak we pulled in behind Petit Bois, a little barrier island off Pascagoula, and anchored so we could clean things up a bit and shower and get some sleep.

After Earl had the boat secured, he broke out the breakfast makings—eggs and sausage and biscuits and cheesy shrimp grits—and we ate on deck, watching the smokestacks over at Standard Oil burning off like candles in a birthday cake.

Willie said he thought he might cast a little for speckled trout before he turned in, and I thought that was a good idea too, so after we were finished with breakfast, we dropped the little dingy and set off for the island to fish in the surf. We left Jackson sitting on deck with Earl, who was working on a six-pack of beer, the form he said he liked his cereal in.

After a couple of hours we got back to the boat with a short stringer of specks, which we figgered Earl could fry up for supper. When we reached the stern and got ready to climb on board, we heard Earl's voice. It was loud. I couldn't see Earl, but I could see Jackson standing just outside the wheelhouse. He had his back to me.

"Look, you cut out that Jesus crap and do your work and you'll get back to land. Otherwise we'll throw your ass overboard. Like Jonah. The sea don't need to be no calmer, but it might improve the shrimping."

Jackson squinted up into the red sun, then looked at Earl. "It really don't matter what you do to me, the Lord'll deliver me, the Lord'll serve me in my time of need as I have served Him."

"The Lord," Earl yelled, "will serve your ass to the fishes."

At that I banged an oar against the side of the boat to let'm know we were close enough to hear, and they shut up. Then we climbed on board. Earl was standing there so mad he was trembling, and Jackson disappeared inside to shower or shit or go to bed.

"I am so tired of hearing about Jesus," he said to us when we had pulled up stools and broken out beers. "He kept telling me that all we got to do is get down in some kinda cluster-fuck circle-jerk and hold hands and pray about it, and the nets'll haul in more shrimp than we can handle. I told him I had always done OK without that and would again, so he could just do his praying on his own."

"I wish he'd get busy," Willie said, "cause we shonuff need some shrimps in them freezers."

I looked at him. "How would a Jew go about improving the yield?"

We all had a good laugh at that and then lined up for a shower.

Late in the afternoon, after we got everything ready to trawl, Earl dropped the anchor inside Dauphin Island, off the Alabama coast, and fried up the specks, which Willie had cleaned earlier, along with some potato spears and hushpuppies. Beer and ice cream for dessert.

After we were through eating, we were sitting on pick stools drinking beer when Jackson, who'd been marveling at how many stars he could see out there during the drags when we were a long way from any kind of major city glare, just up and said, "J'all ever see the Southern Cross?"

I shook my head no. So did Willie. Earl just looked at him, waiting to see what he would say next.

"Well, I have."

I didn't know what to say to that, and neither apparently did Willie, but Earl did.

"Where at?"

Jackson smirked, took a swig from his beer, and pointed his bottle to the southeast.

"The Keys."

"*What* Keys?" Earl asked him.

"The Florida Keys. Key West, you know. You know where that's at."

"Goddamn right I know where it's at, but I also know that you can't see the Southern Cross from any place in the Northern Hemisphere, and that includes the Goddamn Keys."

Jackson snorted. "Can too."

"No, hell, you can't, dumbass."

"With all due respect, Captain, that's bullshit. Jimmy Buffett sings about seeing the Southern Cross, and he's from there, does his sailing down there."

"Jimmy Buffett is from Mobile, Alabama, and he has sailed all over the fucking world, including around Cape Horn and Cape Agulhas, and if you don't know where those are, then get you a Goddamn chart and look'm up. Let's just say that if you sail much farther south than them, you better have a bunch of dogs and a sled handy."

"Where's Cape Agulhas?" Willie asked. "I know that Cape Horn is the southernest part of South America."

"Cape Agulhas is the southernmost part of Africa."

"Did y'all know that Jesus is 'sposed to come back thoo the Southern Cross?"

Neither of us said anything for a little bit. I mean, what the hell is there to say?

"I didn't know that," Earl finally said.

"By the way, how do you know Jimmy Buffett has sailed around them capes?" Jackson just didn't know when to shut up.

"Because I was with him," Earl said, and that pretty much put the issue to bed, though he gave me a wink when he got up and went into the wheelhouse.

Our drags that night weren't much more productive than the ones earlier in the week, so Earl said we'd lay up in the Mississippi Sound for the day and then head to Florida waters middle of the afternoon and set up and drag over there. We had enough provisions and fuel on board for another couple of days and nights, and then we'd have to go into port for a couple of days, which was sure as hell fine with me. I needed some time with a woman.

So we anchored the next morning just inside Petit Bois Island, where you can see the Standard Oil Refinery, if the pollution's not too heavy—I just love watching them smokestacks blazing at the top. Just makes me feel warm and fuzzy, you know.

We had finished our chores and had one of Earl's big breakfasts and cleaned ourselves up a little bit. Willie usually just jumped in the water and swam around, lathering with a bar of soap, then climbed on board and rinsed off in the shower. Said it saved water and was more fun, and Earl was sure as hell for saving fresh water. I was more conventional and took a regular shower.

Well, I had stripped down, took a couple of swigs of the Jack Daniels I kept under my mattress and sprawled out for a few hours of shuteye when that damn Jackson came in and squatted down beside my bunk.

"Jim, you awake?"

"I ain't been laying here but two minutes, so of course I'm awake. What?"

"Jim." His voice was low and secretive. Willie was kicked back in a lounge chair with Earl on deck.

"Jim, I seen something out there late yesterday afternoon on one of the drags, just before dark, something in the water alongside the boat, and I thought I'd talk to you about it."

"What? What the fuck did you see?" I didn't open my eyes. I wasn't giving him that satisfaction.

He leaned in until I could feel his breath on my ear, which

was way too close to suit me, but I didn't roll away from him or anything, just kept my eyes closed and listened. He was whistling through his nostrils, which I hate.

"Jim, man, I think that I seen—I believe that I seen Jesus in the water by the boat."

Well, Goddamn, when somebody says something that outrageous to you, you can't for your life keep your eyes closed and go on listening. Some sort of reflex sets in and your eyes not only snap open like they're spring-loaded and been tripped, but your head jerks so that when you focus you are staring straight at the person that has finally got your attention, looking right up into the tufts of hair in his nose that he makes that whistling sound through. It's like your daddy coming into your room just as you're drifting off to sleep and telling you very calmly that he has just cut your mother into roasts and packaged her for the freezer. You have to *look* at him to see whether your eyes can pick up something that your ears have not.

So I found myself leaping from the dark inside of my eyelids, where I was studying those little veins that dance around like summer lightning, to the red-rimmed eyes of Jackson, quicker than a wink.

"You saw *what*? *Who*?" I was calm, for some reason, and surprised that I wasn't yelling at him.

He eased closer. "Don't say nothing to Earl or Willie, but I believe that I seen Jesus swimming along beside the boat."

"Aw, come on, Jackson. Get your head straight and take a shower and get yourself some rest. You ain't sleeping enough."

He didn't say anything else, just got up and went into the head, and in a few seconds I heard the water running.

Shit, I couldn't sleep after that, so I took another swig of whiskey and went out to where Earl and Willie were laying in the sun. They were talking, so I figgered they wasn't asleep.

I drug up a pick stool beside them.

"Y'all know what that crazy sonofabitch just told me?"

"No telling," Willie said.

"Well, he said that he was looking over the rail during one of the drags late yesterday, and he saw Jesus swimming alongside the boat."

"The shit he did," Willie said, "Jesus His Own Self?"

Earl laughed. "First thing I'd wonder is why the hell was he swimming alongside a ordinary shrimp boat in the Gulf of Mexico off the Mississippi Coast." He laughed again. "How come He wudn't running? I mean, He couldn't keep up *walking* alongside the boat, but He could if He was running. If He could *walk* on water, He could sure as hell *run* on it. Hell, if I'd a'known He was out there, I'd of give Him a ride."

Then Jackson stepped out of the wheelhouse, dripping from his shower, and stormed over to where we were huddled.

"You scoffers are going to regret making fun of me. You are all three going to hell."

"Jackson," Willie said, "I thought you said Jesus was coming back through the Southern Cross, not on no damn shrimp net."

"Well, you can just take me to the dock. I'm not going to stay out here with a bunch of nonbelievers. Just you wait, damn you, when He does come back, y'all will find out how wrong you were."

Earl set his beer down and give him a hard look.

"Looky here, Durwood, you fucking Jesus freak, whether we are right or wrong, I ain't hauling your ass over to Pascagoula or anyplace else until we are through with this Goddamn run, which at the rate we're going might be a week from now. If I have to go in for fuel, I'll dump you on the dock, but you signed on for this trip, and, by God, you are going to work on this deck until we are through."

"You can't make me work on this boat. If I want off, I'll get off. I'll just swim over there to the island and hitch a ride to the mainland."

"Good luck with that," I said. "You might be out here without food or water for several days."

"I'll take my chances, rather than work with you heathen."

"Son," Earl said quietly, "I am the captain of this boat, and you signed on for the trip. You are going to work on this deck till we go back to port with a reasonable load of shrimp onboard. You might not like it, but that's what's going to happen. I'm not going to let you make a fool of yourself and swim to that island without food or water, and I'm damn sure not gonna give you either one to take with you. Now, you settle your ass down and get some rest. We gonna be pulling out of here in a few hours, and you need to get some rest."

"Yeah," Willie said, "and be sure'n rest your *eyes.*"

At that Jackson flung his towel over the railing and stormed back into the wheelhouse and slammed the housing quarters door behind him.

"That towel," Earl said, "is gonna cost him five bucks from whatever pay he's got coming."

Then I told'm I believed I'd try to nap on deck, leave Jackson to his problems. I drug up a lounge chair and flattened it and stretched out to get whatever sleep I could before Earl roused us to head out again.

It was a nice day, sunny, with a light breeze out of the south, so sleeping was easy. We worked in the sun enough that we didn't worry about sunburning—hell, we were all the color of a saddle anyhow. So we snoozed off and on for several hours before Earl stirred and got up and said he reckoned it was about time to wet the nets again. He went into the wheelhouse, and I pulled in the anchors.

Willie went in and woke Jackson up, and, man, he was in a sour mood. The rest of us had fried Spam sandwiches, which Earl threw together, but Jackson mixed up some kinda Jesus food shit in a bowl and ate it, sipping out of that thermos he'd brought. We never did figure out what was in it, but he took a few sips out of it every time he ate. Either he wasn't drinking much out of it each time, or he was refilling it somehow. Whatever, I never saw him drink anything else but an occasional beer. I made up my mind that while he was busy on deck the next time, I was gonna sneak in and see what was in it.

"You get any sleep?" I asked him when he finished his bowl of whatever.

"A little. I mostly prayed for your three hell-bound souls."

"Fuck you, Jackson. Get your ass ready to drop the nets."

He was in a surly mood the whole rest of the afternoon and into the night. When the three of us were having some fried fish for supper, he went inside and probably ate some more of his Jesus food and had some of whatever it was in that damn thermos. Fuck him.

We were in the middle of a drag somewhere off the coast of Alabama, well outside Dauphin Island, when it happened. We had cleaned up the deck and were taking a break. Willie was sitting on the stern with a beer, dangling his legs over the side the way he liked to do, and I was sprawled back in one of the deck chairs looking for satellites. Jackson had gone back inside for something. He hadn't said a damn word all evening.

Then there was a loud *boom* in the wheelhouse, and the engines backed off to idle.

"What the fuck!" Willie spun around and jumped off the stern and had started toward the wheelhouse when Jackson stepped out with the shotgun Earl kept in the cabin.

"You ready for Hell, Willie? Earl's waiting for you." The sonofabitch had that shotgun leveled at Willie. I don't think he even saw me, since the deck chair was facing away from him.

Then there was a long flash and the sound of that shotgun, and Willie slammed back against the stern and settled out flat, arms and legs flailing. In another couple of seconds, I was over the railing and pressed up against the side of the boat.

"Where the fuck are you, Jim?" Jackson was banging the shotgun on the rail right above me.

I didn't dare move. I treaded water and kept my face and

hands pressed against the hull while he went completely around the deck banging that Goddamn shotgun.

"Come on, show yourself, Jim. You need to get on to Hell with your buddies. God give me the order—y'all all gotta die. You wanna come on up here and pray with me and give your soul to the Lord, we might can make a deal. Come on back up here, and let's pray."

Shit. No way I was gonna take a chance with salvation with a crazy sonofabitch who'd just killed two men and still had at least three shells left in that shotgun. I could tread water a long damn time if I had to. But what the hell was he going to do now? Kick up that throttle and leave me swimming out there at least three miles from shore or keep watching until I made some kind of move so that he could get a shot at me? I didn't know. The next move was his. I didn't have any left.

After a long while he quit banging around and it sounded like he went into the wheelhouse, where he was throwing shit around. Then he shut the engine off.

I decided that I'd swim out in front of the boat where he couldn't see me and see what I could make out of what he was doing. What I was hoping was that he would shoot *hisself* and go on off to Heaven or wherever the hell he was headed. Then I'd climb back on board and head to port. Jesus Christ, what a damn mess this was turning into.

I eased along the hull and swam out from the bow a few yards and studied the boat. Everywhere I looked there was nothing but stars, them above and them reflected by the black water. The only sound was the slapping of waves against the boat and an occasional bump or slam from somewhere inside.

The water was cold, but bearable, and I knew that if I had to I could strip down and make it to Dauphin, which lay behind me. The lights from the island gave off a glow good enough to guide me. It would be a long damn haul, but I was a good swimmer and in real good shape. I just couldn't decide what to do for the time being. That was a long swim, and I might not make it. If Jackson would just go on and kill hisself, which I was pretty sure he was going to do, then I'd have the boat to myself. With a crew of three dead guys.

He was still banging around in the wheelhouse. I couldn't imagine what the hell he was doing. All I could see was the outline of the boat with the running lights we had on—that big old bow was blocking everything. So I swam a bit until I could see onto the deck. I was far enough out that he wouldn't be able to see me, and if he did, I hoped I'd be out of range of that damn shotgun. The deck looked like a little stage, with a few footlights and some dangling in the rigging lighting it up.

In a bit I saw Jackson stumbling onto the deck with something he was carrying and bumping along. He bent over a couple of times, and then he straightened out and started taking a fucking bath. He was pouring water from some kind of container and sloshing it all over his legs and torso and arms, and then he lifted a bowl and poured it over his shoulders. Goddamndest thing.

I started easing in closer, since it was obvious that he had given up the hunt for me. He was singing. And then I smelled it. That wasn't water he was bathing in—it was diesel fuel. What the fuck? The sonofabitch had soaked hisself with diesel fuel and started singing right there on deck, arms spread, his face up to the sky. I heard something that sounded like "Just as I am, without one plea." I remembered it from church when I was a boy.

I swam closer. This was some weird shit on top of weird shit and getting weirder by the minute. His voice drifted out over the dark water.

> *Think about how many times*
> *I have fallen*
> *Spirits are using me*

larger voices callin'.
What heaven brought you and me
Cannot be forgotten.
I have been around the world,
Lookin' for that woman girl,
Who knows love can endure.
And you know it will.
And you know it will.

Then he turned around toward me, but there was no way he could see me. With his arms spread, face to the sky, his voice rose, louder and louder.

When you see the Southern Cross
For the first time
You understand now
Why you came this way
'Cause the truth you might be runnin' from
Is so small.
But it's as big as the promise
The promise of a comin' day.
So I'm sailing for tomorrow
My dreams are a dyin'.
And my love is an anchor tied to you
Tied with a silver chain.
I have my ship
And all her flags are a flyin'
She is all that I have left
And music is her name.

Hell, he wasn't a bad singer for sure. I mean, this was some kind of surreal shit going on, with two dead buddies on the boat and me floating around in that dark water and that crazy sonofabitch standing on that rocking stage belting out "Southern Cross" without missing a word of it, that I could notice anyhow.

Then he grabbed up a couple water bottles tied together with a string or something and slung them around his neck and started climbing into the rigging. Climbed right up as high as the foot cleats would let him, and then he started singing again, just bellowing out across the dark water.

> *Think about how many times*
> *I have fallen*
> *Spirits are using me*
> *larger voices callin'.*
> *What heaven brought you and me*
> *Cannot be forgotten.*
> *I have been around the world,*
> *Lookin' for that woman girl,*
> *Who knows love can endure.*
> *And you know it will.*
> *And you know it will.*
> *So we cheated and we lied*
> *And we tested*
> *And we never failed to fail*
> *It was the easiest thing to do.*
> *You will survive being bested.*
> *Somebody fine*
> *Will come along*
> *Make me forget about loving you.*
> *At the Southern Cross.*

He damn sure knew all the words to the song, the best I could tell. Then he hushed and took the bottles from around his neck. Since he had left the shotgun on deck, I swam in close, and I could see him pretty well in the glow of the deck lights, but I couldn't tell what all he was doing. He poured whatever he had in the bottles over his shoulders, first one bottle, then the other. It dribbled down the cables and ropes, and I could see it dripping and drizzling onto the deck. I could smell it then, diesel fuel and gasoline, from the can we used to run the backup generator.

What the bloody fuck?

He untied the bottles and took the cord he had used to tie them together and tied it to the mast and it looked like he ran it around his neck, and then he took something else he had hanging around his neck and held it out in his hand and—the next thing I saw was a spark and a flash. And then *swoosh!* A ball of fire went straight up and a Goddamn sheet of flame shot down onto the deck and across it, and I could see the dark shape of him just splayed there, his legs and arms spread out in the rigging and thrashing, outlined in fire, everything on fire, the whole damned boat stage on fire. And him still singing about the Southern Cross.

When I figgered I was far enough away to be safe, I stopped swimming and turned around and treaded water. The whole boat was a sheet of orange flame against the night sky from the deck up, and there, up in the rigging, that crazy sonofabitch was hanging there, his arms spread, with fire feeding on him like it was hungry for the taste of human flesh.

I didn't know what to do. Didn't know whether the boat would explode or not. There wasn't a whole hell of a lot to burn, since the hull deck was made out of sheet steel, so I figured the fire would burn itself out after a bit.

I swam over and grabbed hold of one of the lines trailing down from a boom to a net and just hung there while the fire burned away. It was intense as hell, but there wasn't no way I was turning loose of them lines. I could see a couple of lights on the water not too many miles off, and I figured they were boats coming toward me to check out the flames, but they never did.

The fire burned a long time. I had no fucking idea what time it was, since I generally didn't wear a watch while we were working on deck, but it had to of been somewhere on over in the early morning. I just hung onto the lines and waited for the sun.

It was a long damn night or morning or whatever it was, but finally I could see the east starting to light up across the whole horizon. The boat was between me and the sun, so well before it had pushed up, I could see the outline of the mast and rigging. And Jackson.

He must of used a piece of wire to tie his neck to the mast, because he was still hanging there, head drooped over, his arms splayed like Jesus on the Cross, his fingers with death grips on the rigging, his legs hanging straight down. His clothes had completely burned away, and as the sun rose and lit up the world, Jackson hung dead in the middle of it, a black husk outlined in gold, his arms spread as if in appeal to some higher, greater power to come and take him home.

Excerpt from Pompeii Man

The following is an excerpt from my novel Pompeii Man, *the story of a honeymoon trip to New Orleans, during which, because of the husband's foolish fantasy, the wife is abducted, raped, and sodomized. The excerpt from Chapter VIII is set on Horn Island on their first real date; Chapter XIX is set on the island after New Orleans. Pompeii Man is Susie's nickname for Stafford, based on his early interest in the doomed city.*

FROM CHAPTER VII

At eleven-thirty that Saturday morning, they were passing due east of Round Island in the Mississippi Sound off Pascagoula, humming along in a little sixteen-foot power-boat toward the south and the dark line of trees of Horn Island. Jerry Harmon's sailboat was out of service for a couple of weeks, but Stafford had no objection to taking the boat they were in. There was more room in it, for one thing, allowing him to stash fishing gear, a picnic basket, an extra cooler of ice, a five-gallon container of water, other odds and ends, and a pup-tent, which he liked to have along on his island trips for gear storage or for shelter if it rained, or perhaps for other things.

Susie was riding in the middle seat, just in front of him, leaning this way and that as swells tilted the boat. She pointed at landmarks as they made their way down the river and out into the Gulf, and he shouted out what he knew of them: the Highway 90 bridge, Ingalls Shipbuilding, the causeway that curled out to the recently completed Naval base just south of Ingalls, now equipped with a cruiser and two frigates. Intrigued with Round Island and its stone lighthouse as it slid by on the left, she leaned back and asked whether they might tour it one day.

"Sure," he yelled over the engine noise. "It's small, but it's very pretty. Lots of trees, but not much beach. And the lighthouse, of course. We can come out anytime you'd like. Horn's much more interesting. Bigger. Lots of game on it. Inland pools with fish and oysters. Got everything."

She shouted something and turned back toward the long flat line of Horn. The wind billowed her white overshirt, tied by its tails around her waist. Beneath that she wore a red tee-shirt, through which, he noticed earlier, her nipples prominently thrust. Ribbons of her hair, the color of sea oats, spilled out from under the little white cap she wore and streamed golden in the sun.

In a larger boat Stafford could have swung around to the east and gone through Horn Island Pass, which separates the larger island from Petit Bois, then headed west and anchored on a shoal, using a stern anchor buried in the sand on the beach for stability. The trip through the waist-deep water of the surf would be easy enough. That would be preferable to unloading all their gear on the inside beach and carrying it over dunes of deep sand nearly half a mile to the Gulf side, where with the sea breeze they would have no concern for mosquitoes and gnats and where the water was crystal clear as it rolled in from the south. The view would be better and the swimming delightful on the outside.

He knew, though, that the pass, choppy at all times and heaving with ground swells, would hammer them pretty hard, perhaps even make Susie ill, so he elected to beach the small boat on the inside and carry everything across. It wouldn't take that long, and a lot of the gear he could wait to unload later, if they needed it at all.

When they ran out of dark water, he puttered slowly into the shallows, cut his engine, and allowed their momentum to carry them to shore. After unloading the equipment he wanted to take across, he dragged the boat as far up the beach as he could and stretched out the bow line and hitched it to a solid stump jutting from the sand. No matter what the tide or wind did, the boat would go nowhere.

Balancing one of the ice chests on his shoulder, he walked Susie over to find a good campsite. She carried a roll of blankets and towels under one arm and the pup-tent under the other, dangling from her right hand a bright red canvas travel bag.

"That was rough." She stepped in his footprints on the warming sand, which tapered up to the first line of dunes.

"Lots of open water. That sailboat would probably have been a little smoother, but we'd still be five miles out."

"You really think the tent's necessary, huh?" she asked him as they struggled to the top of a dune studded with palmettos. Before them lay a smaller line of dunes and beyond those a flat stretch of sand that led to the rolling blue-green waters of the Gulf.

"Well," he grunted, shifting the ice chest to his other shoulder, "it's a good storage place for all your stuff, keeps the blowing sand off of it, and if it rains, you can always crawl up inside it for shelter."

"I guess couples a little farther along in their relationship could do other things in it too, huh?" They had started walking again.

He stopped and looked at her, above him on the downward slope of the path. "Yeah, I guess so. I suppose it would be nice of me to say that I never thought of that."

"It would be nice," she said, grinning, "but it would be a lie, wouldn't it?"

God, he thought, turning back down the path, *this girl's got me so off-balance I can barely keep my breath.*

He stumbled, then righted himself. *Or maybe it's this God-damned ice chest.*

"Know what I forgot?" she asked.

"What?" He stopped and turned around.

"A camera."

"Brought your sketchpad, didn't you?"

"Yes." She patted the red bag. "It's in here."

He shifted the ice chest to his other shoulder.

"That's better than a camera."

"You think so?"

"Sure. A camera can't interpret, can't improve on what it sees. Do you think people would buy Anderson's or Smithers' stuff if they had just taken pictures? It's how *they* saw what they painted and sketched that matters. Their *interpretation* of what was before them. Maybe you'll find something nice out here, sketch it, or paint it."

Then they topped another dune and stood looking out onto the outer beach, beyond which the Gulf spread off to the skyline.

"Maybe so," she said.

They chose a spot on the sand well out of reach of the surf at high tide, one easily determined by the darker swirled patterns formed by water action on the last high tide as the waves swept in, lost their momentum, and returned. Every way he looked, there was trash from island visitors and jetsam from trolling fishing boats and freighters farther at sea: beer cans and plastic wrappers, jugs and bottles and buckets, pieces of nylon rope, limbs and trunks of trees from God only knew where and timbers of all sizes, some thick as a horse.

Smithers and Anderson simply blocked it out, he thought, *didn't see it*. He hoped she was not put off by the panorama of trash.

If it weren't for the great storms that roared in off the Gulf every few years, flushing away the debris of ships and summer idlers, the trash would be intolerable. Nature had her way of cleansing, though, hurling massive storm surges against man's petty fouling and leaving the beaches pure and clean again.

He had walked Horn after a hurricane and found not a single can or bottle or snarl of rope on the sand, just shells and sand dollars where the sea had emptied her pockets. Like in the beginning, like the sun rising on the first day of the spinning mottled world.

Stafford suggested to Susie that she walk along the beach while he brought the rest of their stuff across the island. The picnic basket and his fishing gear would pretty well do them for now. If he fished and caught enough to take back, he could always go get the other ice chest.

"When you are out of sight, I'm going to change into my bathing suit, if you don't mind." She nodded toward the red bag beside the rolled-up tent. "You won't look?"

"No. But take care that you don't draw a bunch of boats in here and mess up the fishing."

She laughed. "I'll be quick." She unbuttoned her shorts even before he had dropped behind the first dune.

When he returned with the fishing gear and picnic basket, she was waist deep in the surf, her hands out flat on the surface of the water to either side, as if she were trying to lift herself by them. Swells washed over her shoulders as she braced against them. What an absolutely perfect figure she had, and how white and fine her skin was. He stripped down to his cutoffs and waded out to her.

"I don't want to be bossy, but did you put on sunscreen?" he asked.

"Yes. Can't you smell it?"

When he bent until his nose almost touched her shoulder he detected a faint coconut fragrance.

"Yes. Sorry. You're just so fair, I was—I just thought I'd warn you."

She turned and faced him. The bill of the little white cap was turned to the side. "How do you know I'm fair? We haven't played a game yet."

"God, you're cute," he said, reaching out to take her hands. The top of her black two-piece was amazingly thin, so that her nipples stood out clearly in its wet sheen. "No, you're beautiful. No, you're *incredible*. No—"

"You don't have much body hair," she said, running her hand across his chest.

"I'm higher up the ladder of evolution. If I had hair all over my chest and back, I'd already have swept you up and lugged you back into the dunes and ravished you, perhaps eaten you for dinner."

"Wouldn't you have to club me first or something?"

"No," he intoned. "I like my women alert and kicking."

"Hmmmm." She reached and ran her hand over his right shoulder and down onto his biceps. "I guess you could do it." She laughed and kissed him lightly on the cheek. "Come on, let's go eat. I'm starving." She pulled him toward the sand.

"Can I kiss you first?" he asked, holding back.

"I just kissed you first. How can—"

He grasped her around the waist and pressed his body to hers, softly kissing at first, then kissing harder and deeper, until she gasped and pulled away.

"Jack, slow down, please. We've got the whole afternoon for things to run their course. You say you are a gentleman, and I believe you. Don't mess this up. I came out here with you to have fun on the island, but that doesn't necessarily mean the sort of fun that men usually have in mind. Slow it down. It's our first date, remember."

She started pulling him toward the beach again. "Come on, let's eat."

Stafford was surprised at how easily he backed off, allowing her to lead. He wasn't accustomed to this coyness. The older women he dated generally wanted sex as much as he did, and they had no reservations about it: one or the other led and the other responded. Everything was so spontaneous, almost as it had been in the seventies, when free love was sweeping college campuses, though he knew that the reason he was successful so often and so quickly was that he chose well whom to approach. He almost never messed around with anyone much younger than he was, and he had a keen eye for picking women who needed the deep, slow love of a capable man.

He was cautious about AIDS, far more common among the young; but much more important, he preferred older women because they knew how to make love, something he himself had only in recent years learned, and he had learned it from them, from lonely older women, women life had already wounded. They knew, and they taught him, that there were two people involved and that the outer boundaries of lovemaking were established by the limits of the imagination of the two people making it.

College girls, and he had had a few of them, couldn't mellow into a relationship. They played their silly little games, and their lovemaking was shallow, then afterwards they felt that you were obligated to them, bound to them, as if some sort of social contract had been formed from a mere coupling. He wanted women with a past, women who became someone other than themselves, or maybe became what they *really* were, for that brief period of lovemaking, who loved wildly, almost savagely, as if they never could quite satisfy their longing, and then closed the door softly when they left, their faces and clothes in order, and waited for *you* to call; or if they called you, they were discreet and—dare he say it?—*professional* about it. No entanglements, no complications. The one sex partner he steadily turned to was Emily Miller. The other two were just now-and-then wham-bams, one who had endured a dreadful marriage to an arrogant husband, a superintendent at the shipyard who was a bastard in every respect and for whom he felt nothing but contempt as he made his wife writhe and moan, the other a widow five years his senior who worked for a drugstore in Ocean Springs. None of them pressured him, ever, and he felt comfortable with them. They would call or drop by, set a date and time, then show up ready for action.

They had lunch on the beach, using the ice chest as a table between them.

"Wow, the stuff you've got in here," she'd said when she took out their pimento cheese sandwiches. "Cokes and beer, a bottle of wine, milk, juice, bags of fruit . . . and salad makings? How many days did you say we're we staying?"

"I like to come prepared," Stafford answered. "I might catch a redfish or two and we can cook them on the beach for dinner."

"Can you make that run across the Sound after dark, with those cork things everywhere—crab-trap markers, you called them? Will it be safe?"

"We can get into the river before dark. You don't have to be back early, do you?"

She had laid out one of the towels over the ice chest, putting a sandwich and sweating Coke at each end, with napkins.

"No, not really. I told Polly—my roomie, you remember— that I'd probably be in before eight, but it's no big deal. You wanted Coke, didn't you?"

"Beer, actually, but you've already got the Cokes out, so Coke'll be fine."

After lunch he put on his shirt and wedged an old Aussie hat onto his head, she slipped her white overshirt and cap on, and after reapplying sunscreen—he wanted to ask her to let him rub hers on, but didn't—and they headed west on the beach.

Stafford had strapped on his fishing knife, shoved a plastic box of lures into a back pocket of his cutoffs, and shouldered his rod. From midsummer on into late fall, redfish fed in the gullies that stretched out finger-like from the beach, sometimes singles or two or three, sometimes great schools of them appearing as red blobs in the crystal water as the mass of fish moved along, vague scarlet ghosts, with here and there a big bull or female working the flanks. Catching one was a simple matter of easing to the edge of the water and flinging a lure out beyond the mass of fish and reeling it back through them. In their feeding frenzy one would snatch the bait and the fight to the beach began, sometimes lasting for several minutes as you cranked, pulled, cranked and pulled, until, exhausted, he rode a wave up onto the beach and you claimed him. Or the line snapped, which could easily happen using a fifteen-pound line against fish that could weigh well over twenty. Then you had to put another lure on as fast as you could and try to catch up with the red ghosts, always moving, and cast again. Landing a big red should certainly impress Susie, but not as much as having fresh redfish fillets on the beach later. If things worked out the way he intended, this would be a memorable day for the exquisite blond woman whose footsteps he swallowed into his own as they walked in the heavy sand.

In one hand Susie carried her sketchbook, dangling from the other a green plastic bucket she'd found earlier, plunking little oddities into it: shells and sand dollars, an osprey feather. Like a child delirious with discovery, she stayed a few paces ahead of Stafford, turning around now and again to hold up to him some shell she'd found. He walked along watching her motion on the sand, convinced that of all the women walking the world's beaches at that moment, this was the one he wanted with him.

"You didn't set up the tent," she reminded him as the ice chest grew smaller and smaller in the distance. "I thought you were supposed to stash the gear in it."

"The weather's pretty. Wind's mild, no clouds threatening. Everything'll be fine till we get back there."

"OK," she said and returned to her search for shells.

Keeping even a remote corner of his mind on fishing was difficult, but when he saw at the edge of his vision a couple of large fish moving across a bright sandy shoal from one finger of dark water into another, he snapped back to the real world and lunged past Susie to take a position just ahead of where the fish had disappeared into the cut. He hurled the red-headed chartreuse lure at a point beyond where they had dropped off the shoal and just ahead of where he judged them to be.

Susie had stopped her beachcombing to watch as Stafford, standing in water just below his knees, twitched the rod, reeled a few feet in, and twitched again. He was reeling in the second run of slack, fearful that he had misjudged their position, when the fish struck, bowing the rod and stripping out line. With Susie squealing in the background, he tightened the drag ever so carefully, turned the fish, and began working him toward the beach.

Judging by the dogged straight pull, it was a sow or bull red, an easy ten pounds, probably more, and he had to work it slowly, slowly, as the stubborn shadowy fish made a move to the right, then turned back to deeper water, yielded when Stafford bowed back hard on him, then turned to the left and out to sea again.

But he tired quickly, rolled on the surface, and, after one more feeble effort to head back out, began to move compliantly toward the beach. When the red approached the first breakers, Stafford backed out onto the upper beach and allowed a crest to ride the fish out onto the slick sand. In three strides he had their dinner hoisted by the gills.

"Oh, Jack, he's beautiful." She was squinting at the redfish, nearly two feet long, now laid out on the beach beyond the edge of the water, his gills flaring for oxygen in the alien air. She stooped and ran her finger down the middle of his belly, flinching when he flapped his tail against the sand.

"A dozen pounds, I'd guess, maybe fifteen." He removed the hook with a twist. "Lotta good eating here."

"What'll we do with him now?" she asked.

"I probably ought to try to catch another one or two, some to take back, but I don't want a whole lot to clean, so I'll just lug him to the campsite and go across for the other ice chest. You go ahead and walk on up the beach and when I've got him filleted and stashed on ice I'll join you. You should find something to sketch." He shaded his eyes toward the west.

"I don't see anybody else, no boats anchored along there anywhere, so you should have it to yourself."

"What if I get lost?"

"You won't. Stay on the beach and you won't. But even if you leave it for something, I'll just follow your tracks. You won't get lost." He hoisted the fish and headed down the beach to the campsite.

When he joined her well over an hour later and perhaps two miles up the beach, following her tracks where they dipped down onto the tide slick, then turned up into the white, loose sand of the upper beach, Susie was sitting on the top of a dune staring off toward the middle of the island, where even before he rose to her level Stafford could see a flock of buzzards massed in a sandy stretch of palmettos. Earlier he had seen some of them spiral down, so he knew something was dead over there. Decades before, buzzards had flown in great flocks out to the islands to roost in the evenings, but a cholera epidemic among hogs on the island and mainland had so reduced the scavengers' population that it was now uncommon to see many on Horn. In fact, he could not recall ever having seen more than one or two circling out over the Gulf.

She had her sketchbook on her lap, beside her the green bucket.

"Jack, what do you suppose they've got?" she asked as he panted up.

"Dunno. Maybe a hog. There are a few wild pigs out here. Maybe an alligator. Whatever it is, it isn't feeling a thing, and they're having a hell of a meal. Too bad we've eaten."

"Yeah, too bad. Do you think maybe we ought to check it out, in case it's some*body*?" She was clutching her little green bucket of shells. She had been in the water—sand clung to her legs up to her bathing suit.

"I'll walk over there if you want me to and look, but it's just some animal they've got. Bet on it."

He looked over her shoulder. "Whatcha drawing?"

She held the pad up. He could recognize trees and palmettos, some small clouds, and heaving shrub-studded dunes. She had blushed the trees and shrubs with pale chalk and swept the sky with blue. The gauzy little clouds seemed to follow each other obediently, like sheep. A pair of pelicans flew, wingtips nearly touching, just above her dunes.

"Where are the buzzards?" he asked her.

"I don't see them. I see past them, through them. I see trees and sky and dunes. And gulls. The buzzards remind me too much of death."

"You've drawn the pelicans well."

He tapped the page with his finger. "Brown pelicans. Beautiful birds."

"Is that what they are? I thought they were gulls."

"Oh, much rarer. Much nobler than common gulls. They'd be offended if they knew you thought they were gulls."

"Please don't tell them."

She was so incredibly lovely sitting there atop the dune, her hair trailing out in the sea breeze, that Stafford had to keep reminding himself to go slow. Jesus, he wanted to kiss her.

He smiled. "Not a word to them. You've done a great job with this."

Then he pointed to the cluster of buzzards. "Now I'm going over there to find out what the guys in the black suits are having for lunch."

He scrambled down from the dune and struck out through scattered palmettos and low-growing shrubs he could not identify toward the mass of dark birds, whose shuffling and clacking he could hear at some distance.

"Mind if I go along?"

She had come up behind him, still wagging her green bucket. She had the pad clamped under her arm.

"It might not be pleasant," he warned.

Well before he reached the spot, the buzzards broke like a clap of thunder and rose in different directions to circle, their heavy wings whistling and buffeting. Their shadows rippled over the dunes. Some settled in the larger trees that ran down the middle of the island; others continued to ride down the wind, bank, and flap back into it.

"It's a deer," Stafford said as they approached the place the buzzards had risen from. "A small deer."

The carcass had been stretched out of shape and torn apart, the way wild dogs would have done it, but he could see no evidence in the agitated sand that anything other than buzzards had fed. The deer's swollen tongue lolled onto the sand, as if she were licking salt. Why hadn't the buzzards gone for *it*, he wondered. There was no evidence of a penis, so he assumed that it was a doe, though the entire anal and vaginal area had been eaten away. Upwind of it, he studied the scene, trying to determine what had killed the deer. An occasional crosscurrent swirled the smell in their direction. Susie was holding a hand over her mouth and nose.

"Oh, Jesus, Jack." She pinched her nose and backed up, turning toward the beach. "Let's go. We've seen it. Let's go."

"Too young to have died a natural death, I'd say," he suggested on their way to the beach. "Can't imagine what might have killed it out here. Shouldn't be any hunters around." Behind him he could hear the buzzards fluttering down to their meal.

"I'm not that interested in knowing why it's dead," she said. "You'd never guess from Anderson's sketches and Smithers' paintings that stuff like that was going on out here, would you?"

"They were *selective*," Stafford answered, sweeping his eyes up and down the beach, "as artists must always be."

They made their way slowly east again, hand in hand. Stafford had left his fishing tackle at the ice chest, so he carried the green bucket, holding it out to her whenever she found something she wanted to add to it.

"What'll you do with these?" he asked, shaking the shells around and looking at what she'd collected.

"Don't break my sand dollars, boy." She bumped him with her hip. "I don't know what I'll do with them. Sketch them, maybe. Make a display. Anybody living on the coast ought to have a shell display, don't you think?"

"Absolutely. And these can remind you of the day you spent on Horn Island with a librarian."

"Who doesn't look at all like a librarian." She reached over and pinched his forearm.

They lolled on the beach awhile, so afternoon was well on the wane when they reached camp. After some water and a beer, Stafford suggested that they take a swim and then he'd start a fire to cook the fish. He had put cornmeal, a quart of cooking oil, salt and pepper, and a cast-iron frying pan in the bottom of the picnic basket, and there was plenty of wood along the beach to get a good fire going. Wine, a salad, and fried redfish so fresh that it might still be twitching when he dropped in the pink fillets ought to go a long way toward making Susie feel that this had been a special day. Then, after dinner. . . .

They swam for a while out near the blue-green water of the deeper Gulf that lay a hundred yards or so off the beach. The tide was coming in, so there was no danger of their being carried out to sea, and there was nothing to fear from anything that swam in those waters, notwithstanding the remote possibility that some sort of predator fish might take a swipe at an arm or leg. He'd gotten scratches from bluefish and mackerel, but he had never heard of a shark attack off the islands.

Susie Clayburn swam as gracefully as she walked, taking long, even, balanced strokes, coupled with perfectly timed kicks that propelled her through the water with tireless ease. He swam alongside her, with greater effort to keep up than he had imagined he would need, sometimes passing her just to show that he could do it, then dropping behind again. She seemed not to fear the deeper water at all, at one time veering to her left and thrusting into the oncoming waves with such vigor that he lost sight of her momentarily and was on the verge of calling out when he saw her stroking toward him, face up, smiling.

She did not tire quickly enough for him, so after what seemed well over an hour he suggested that they go back to the beach and have another beer and he'd prepare dinner. The sun had slid far over in the western sky, and the wind, bearing the faintest trace of fall, picked up.

Susie sat on one of the ice chests, sipping a beer and watching him make the fire.

"That water's wonderful." She was still dressed in her bathing suit, but with her shirt on. "I've been in the ocean only a few times in my life."

He grunted as he finished the little sand pit and began laying small strips of driftwood in the bottom, over which he would lace larger limbs as the fire progressed. He still wore only his cutoffs.

"You looked at home out there to *me*. It was all I could do to keep up with you."

"Oh, I've done lots of swimming. Just not in saltwater. It lifts you up so much that you seem to be *skimming* instead of swimming."

When the fire was going to his satisfaction, Stafford opened the second ice chest and removed a fillet, half the redfish, sliced it down the middle, and then cut one of the sections in half. It was still a hell of a chunk of fish. He put the rest back into the ice chest and, using the chest as his kitchen counter, cut the piece into two-inch slices and dropped them into a plastic bag of cornmeal, flavored with salt and pepper. This he shook vigorously until all the pieces were well coated.

"That's a lot of fish," she said.

"Susie, would you mind getting the oil and pan out of the picnic basket?" He thought it a good touch to involve her in making the meal. That way it would be *their* dinner and not *his*. "Pour an inch of oil in the bottom of the skillet."

"You brought a pan and oil and cornmeal? Heavens, Jack Stafford, you really don't forget the tiniest thing, do you?"

He laughed. "I try not to."

He took the skillet from her and set it across a piece of wire mesh he had wrested from a tangle of timbers on his way back to camp after catching the fish and had fashioned into a cradle that would keep the skillet from sliding into the fire. As he waited for the oil to heat up, they spread one of the blankets and put the ice chest they had used for a table at lunch in the middle. Earlier he had taken out the wine and salad bag, whose contents, already drenched with oil and vinegar, he emptied into two bowls from the picnic basket. True, he *had* thought of everything.

When the oil in the skillet began to bubble and roll, he reached for the pieces of fish and carefully slid them in, noting with gratification that they immediately whined and sizzled. He winced at the heat on his face.

"Susie, hand me the tongs from the basket, please," he said as the fillets began to float and tumble.

She rummaged about for a few seconds, finally setting the contents out onto the blanket.

"Better hurry. The fish is getting close. Gotta get'm out of that oil." The smoke from the skillet was blinding him. He hooked a stick through the hole in the handle and slid it to the edge of the fire.

"Jack, there're no tongs in here."

"Then a spatula! Hell, *anything!*"

She pointed to the empty basket. "No tongs, no spatula."

He looked over at the blanket, where everything that had been in the basket was neatly set out. Susie was shrugging, her eyes on the roiling fish.

"Holy shit!" Stafford grabbed the basket and inverted it. Nothing fell out. His eyes lit on the absurd little plastic forks lying alongside a stack of napkins. "Good God Almighty!"

"Your knife, Jack," she yelled, "use your *knife*."

He fumbled with his scabbard, realized the knife wasn't there, and scrambled to the ice chest he'd been using as his cooking table, swooped up the knife and tried to spear the pieces of smoking fish. He flipped the last fillet out onto a paper plate just before it turned completely black, then snatched up the skillet, using his tee-shirt to protect his hand, and set it down away from the fire. He slid the jumble of burned fish onto paper towels on top of the ice chest and sat back on the sand.

"So this is blackened redfish, huh?" she asked as she probed a piece with her plastic fork the way a woman might poke at a dead snake with a stick.

"No, *burned* redfish." He rose to his knees. "Hand me what's left of the oil."

"Please?"

"I'm sorry. Please. I'm sorry I lost my cool and yelled at you. Sorry for swearing."

"Like we'd been married five years," she said, laughing. She passed the bottle of oil to him.

Whatever mood he'd been working on was dashed now. He flung the first pieces of fish out into the dark water and wiped away the black residue from the bottom of the skillet with paper towels.

"Too bad we don't have a dog to feed it to," he said.

She laughed. "No dog would eat it."

Then he laughed too and wrapped the handle with his tee-shirt again, and he poured the rest of the oil in the pan and slid it back onto the wire. As it began to bubble, he carefully dropped in another batch of battered pieces. This time he was ready: When the fish was done on one side, he skillfully trapped the fillets between two long narrow pieces of driftwood and flipped them, allowed them a few minutes on the other side, then scooped them up and out onto paper towels he'd laid out on the ice chest.

All this while neither of them had said anything, though he knew that she must be thinking what a fool he was not to have thought about tongs or a spatula if he was going to fry fish. A woman *would* have thought of it.

"That was a clever solution," she suggested as they laid the ice chest out with their dinner, "using the wood. Not as good as tongs, I guess, but it did the trick."

He blushed. "Well, I thought of just *about* everything." He poured the wine and held a stem out to her.

"Wine glasses he thought of, but not tongs for the fish." She rolled her eyes and laughed.

He held his glass out to her. "Here's to this glorious day."

She clinked hers against his. "Which, by the way, is slipping away pretty fast." She sipped from her glass and nodded toward the west. "We're going to be pushing this thing awfully close, aren't we?"

Ablaze with late fire, the sun was still at least an hour away from dropping into the Gulf, but he knew that she was well aware of the time it would take to carry the gear back across the island and how long the trip was to the mainland and upriver to Jerry Harmon's dock.

"We've still got a lot of sun," he reassured her, "and the afterglow will last a couple of hours. We'll be all right."

They ate then, with the fire cracking and popping at their backs and the sun casting long shadows in the dunes. The tide was still inching up the sand toward them, though they were at least a dozen feet above the high line. She had two pieces of the fish, he had the remaining four, and they finished off the wine.

"Glad it was a big fish," she said, daintily wiping the corners of her mouth when she was through eating. "That would have been tough throwing away all we had because you burned it."

"Yeah," he said, "I planned it that way. Thought it would be entertaining for you."

"It *was*," she said.

When they had finished, she packed the picnic basket and rolled up the blanket while he buried their trash from dinner up in the dunes. Then they stood together on the slick tidal sand and stared out across the darkening water.

"I saw two books in the basket," she said. "How long did you plan for us to stay out here?"

"Oh, I always carry books along, just in case I get a chance to read."

"Mercy, those covers and titles—I wouldn't have figured . . ."

"They're just fun reading for me. Just escape." He kept his face turned from her. "They're a break from serious reading is all."

She looked back toward the coastline. "Jack, we'd better get a move on. The sun's almost gone."

He reached and touched her arm. "Susie, wait a minute."

"Jack, the sun's going down. We've got to get off this island."

"Come here." He sat down at the edge of the water and patted a place for her to sit. "Please."

She came and kneeled beside him. "Jack, what is going on here? It'll take two trips across there to get this stuff to the boat, and then we've got to run across the Sound. It'll be dark before we get there. All those crabtraps. I'm getting nervous."

He stared out over the Gulf and said quietly, "I could carry a load over to the boat and fiddle with the engine and tell you it wouldn't start, that I'd have to wait till morning to see well enough to fix it, could even yank a couple of wires loose so that it really *wouldn't* crank. But that would be lying. The engine's fine and it'll start first pull. I know that. Now *you* know that. But I also know that I want to spend the night out here with you, in that orange tent."

He worked his toes in the wet sand. "If you really do have to get back, I'll do my damnedest to dodge those crab traps and get into the river before it gets full dark. With the running lights and my big flashlight we'll make it just fine. But I really want us to stay out here."

She remained silent, her eyes in the same direction as his.

"I've brought along plenty of provisions for us—the fruit's for breakfast. Milk and orange juice too."

"You know," she said softly, "if you hadn't worked so hard setting all this up, which is in itself a form of lying, of course, and if I hadn't enjoyed this day so much with you, I'd say let's pack up and shoot for the river."

She reached and hooked a hand in one of his. "But, frankly, I think I'd like to stay out here with you. I told Polly that if I didn't get back tonight, it would mean that I had stayed over with you."

He sighed and pulled her to him over the wet sand. "God, you are full of surprises."

"Jack, ground rules. . . ."

He released her. "Susie, I won't do anything that you don't want me to do. OK? You're in charge of that department. You've got my word on it."

"Jack Stafford," she said, rising and pulling him to his feet, "*you* are the one full of surprises. I never thought I'd run across a man like you. You intrigue the hell out of me. I'll spend the night out here with you in that little orange tent, which I haven't even seen unrolled yet, much less set up, and I'll sleep in it right beside you, but sleep is all it will be. Understood?"

"Hey," Stafford said, holding her hands, "it's your ballgame. I'll go as far as you want and no farther."

"Jack," she whispered, touching him on the cheek, "it's not that I don't want to make love to you. I *do*. But I don't need the complication right now, and for me that's what it would be, a complication. I am scared of you, frankly, scared of your experience, your intelligence. You've been to Pompeii, been all over the world, for God's sake. I've never been *anywhere*. The age difference is not a factor, but the experience *is*—you're a man of the world. If I made love to you on this beach tonight, it would just be too complicated for me. I'd feel like you were measuring me against all the women you've had, and apparently you've had plenty. I have played with you, eaten with you, shared several memorable hours with you, but I won't make love to you. In time, maybe, but not yet."

"Well, you're wrong about one thing. I wouldn't measure you against anybody. But it's your game, so to speak. I won't touch you unless you want me to. OK? End of discussion."

"Thanks, Jack. I just wanted to be clear about it."

"You have been," he said.

"It would be an honor to sleep with Pompeii Man in his orange tent." She kissed him lightly on the cheek.

"I will tell you, though, if you had brought along tongs, I would not do this. You would be too much in control. Watching you flail around for something to pick those fillets up with was worth the trip out here, you clumsy man. You had more trouble catching the fish the second time than the first."

They both laughed at that, the experienced man of almost forty who'd been to Pompeii, had been all over the world, who understood and reveled in life's great mysteries, who'd had more girls and women than he could remember, and the young woman just out of her teens who had spent a couple of hours once just across the Mexican border and had perhaps never made love—and he was very glad to be with her on that beach, fading from day into starlit evening, to be sharing whatever it was that they had shared that day and would share that night, even if he could not have her.

When they had finished the last bit of tidying up from dinner, Stafford suggested that he pitch the tent in the dunes to take advantage of the wind, which he knew would shift in the night from south to north as the land mass cooled and the water kept its warmth. The breeze would keep them comfortable and drive away mosquitoes and gnats.

"Do you want me to help?" she asked. "Or is it a man thing?"

"You just enjoy yourself. I'll do it. I've set this thing up so much that I could do it one-handed, in the dark. Won't be a minute."

He selected a spot high above the beach in a valley between two dunes and built a large fire, then carried up the ice chests and picnic basket and finally the tent and blankets, leaving Susie walking on the beach until he had things the way he wanted. He was careful to erect the tent far enough away from the fire that an errant ember would not melt a hole through the nylon. After he had unrolled it and tapped in the stakes, he stretched the guy-lines tight and dug a small trench around the periphery to conduit off rain if it should storm.

When he was finished with the tent, he laid a couple of logs across the fire. There were bits of usable wood everywhere, sun-bleached logs and uprooted stumps abraded by the surf and mahogany and pine timbers used as stacking runners on freighters and jettisoned after offloading cargoes. In seconds the dry wood was wrapped in flame. Susie was waist-deep in the rising water when he returned to the beach.

She waded over to him. "I wish we'd have a full moon."

"Wrong time of month. We'll have nothing but stars."

"Out here I'll bet they light things up almost as much as the moon would, like thousands of little penlights beaming down on us."

"You're good with metaphors and similes, Susie Clayburn," Stafford said, taking her hand.

A late-forming cloudbank had snuffed out the western glow that he had hoped they could enjoy, leaving the water before them a black bulge that stretched out to the horizon, where here and there the small lights of ships inched along.

Finally he said, "I suspect that the sea is where metaphors first came from as some man topped a sandy rise somewhere and beheld a sight such as this, only I doubt that he'd have had much to compare it to."

"I'd figure the stars," she said.

"The stars?"

"Yes, when some woman looked up past the head of the hairy man that had her pinned to the ground, wondering whether any of those holes in the night sky could offer escape."

"Jesus, Susie, where'd you get that?"

"It just came to me. Sorry. Sounds like an indictment, doesn't it? I didn't mean anything by it. I'm minoring in English."

He stared at her face, lit by the faintest trace of light from the west, and shook his head. What an incredible woman he had with him. Twenty-one years old and primed to become whatever he wanted to mold her into. Beautiful, intelligent, clever, marvelous sense of humor. It was almost more than he could believe. And here he was alone on an island with her and would later share her bed.

You have got to be careful with this one, Jack, old boy, you can't let this one get away.

"Do you want to swim?" he asked.

"Sure."

She removed her shirt, neatly folded it, and laid it on the sand. Stafford had put his shirt on a bit earlier. He removed it and laid it beside hers. He wished that he had brought swim trunks. His cutoffs, great for walking along the beach and camping and fishing, were a hindrance in swimming—the pockets filled with water and created drag.

"Susie," he yelled as she moved into the surf, "would you mind if I swam in my undershorts? These cutoffs slow me down."

"No, of course not. You can swim naked, if you want to. It won't bother me."

Damnation, what a woman. What exactly did she have in mind to do with him? She seemed so loose and casual about sexual matters when they talked, but left no doubt where she stood on actually going to bed with him. She was inviting him to swim naked with her, but . . .

"Do you want me to take *my* suit off?" she asked as she came back to the beach. He stood with his cutoffs unbuttoned and unzipped but still clinging to his hips.

"Susie, I just don't understand what is going on. What about the ground rules?"

"Jack, swimming naked with you is not the same as making love to you. I know you won't touch me unless I let you, so we can be naked out here all night and nothing will happen. Right?"

She looked at him for a nod, which he gave. "I like swimming naked. I like *being* naked. Now, if you'll turn around and take your clothes off, I'll take my swimsuit off and we'll swim."

"How close can I get to you?" he said over his shoulder as he dropped his cutoffs in the sand and slid off his jockeys.

"Jack, you won't be able to get close enough to see or touch *anything*." Her rolled-up swimsuit sailed over his head and landed high on the sand just as she swatted him on the buttocks and plunged into the surf, rising up on a wave, stroking toward deep water.

"Susie," he yelled over the tumbling water, "orient yourself on the camp." Behind them the fire burned brightly in the cut between the dunes.

He stood for a moment at the edge of the beach trying to figure out where she was in the darkness before him. Then he saw a flashing arm about twenty yards out and heard her laugh and she was gone.

He plunged toward the spot where he'd seen her and began pulling in long strokes, thrusting with his kicks, but she was not there, nor could he see anything of her when he stopped swimming and treaded water out near the edge of the shelf, beyond which the deep lay. Panic began stirring in his chest as he swam back toward the beach. How in God's name would he handle it if something happened to her out there?

Then the notion struck him that he might find her far out in the waves, exhausted, near drowning, dive and come up behind her, hook an arm around just under her shoulders and ease her back to shore, where he'd bring her back to life and spend the rest of the night making love to her in the tent.

He had just made a turn to the west and slowed to an easy stroke parallel with the beach, his head high out of the water so that he could hear her call, when he felt something brush past his feet, followed by a shrill "Pompeii Man!"

And she was gone again, her arms flashing for an instant before she disappeared into the dark waves. Whatever notions he'd had about touching her, or even seeing her long enough to know what he was seeing, faded as he followed a zigzag course back to the east until he saw to his left the dwindling fire in the dunes. He wasn't swimming with her or after her—he was merely swimming in the same Gulf. Male or not, stronger or not, he was no match for her in that night sea.

After a few minutes, having seen nothing of her and heard nothing but the rush of the sea, he left the water and backed away from the edge of the surf and shouted for her. As good as she was in the water, he was still uneasy.

"Susie!" he yelled, first east, then to the south, then west.

Nothing. Nothing but the hiss and tumble of the surf. He turned and noticed that the fire was almost out, so he gathered bits of driftwood along the way, then climbed to the campsite and fed on increasingly larger limbs until flames leapt higher than his head. Earlier he had pulled up a couple of larger logs, which he laid across the fire to burn in two, giving him an even bigger fire at the moment and leaving the halves for later burning. Driftwood, as wonderful as it was for campfires, burned with fast heat and light and was done too soon.

The fire now cast a glow all the way to the beach. Stafford walked back down to the water's edge and yelled again, in all three directions, getting no reply but the steady beat of the surf. He knew nothing else to do, so he struck off to the west along the beach, realizing suddenly that he was still naked. All the while he was building up the fire he simply didn't notice.

"My God," he said quietly to himself, "how the hell can you not notice that you're buck-ass *naked*? What if I come up on somebody out here? They'll think I'm crazy."

He was glad it was not dead summer, when other people might be camping along the eastern tip of Horn. A couple of hundred yards down the beach he turned toward the sea and yelled again and again and got no reply but the mocking surf. *Swish, gone—swish, lost—swish, gone—swish.*

"Jesus," he said to the tumbling black water, "what in the name of all the gods of the sea am I going to do?"

He cupped his hands and shouted her name again and again in all directions. Maybe she was off in the dunes relieving herself. He dropped his hands to his sides and stood staring out at the enormous Gulf. The dancing fire threw jags of light across the sand. Or maybe she was playing with him.

Stafford walked down the beach to the west and raised his face and shouted again, this time with as much force as he could muster and with an edge of anger to his voice.

"Susie! Susie, if you can hear me, answer me, please. This has gone on long enough. Susie!"

"Ja-a-a-a-ck."

The voice came low and ghostly from a higher ledge of sand to his right, and he spun and crouched back on the heels and raised his arms. He widened his eyes to draw in more light and swept them across the stretch of sand and then he saw her. She stood halfway between the water and first line of dunes, her body faintly outlined against the white background.

"Susie, what are—"

"You couldn't catch me in the water, Pompeii Man. Can you catch me in the *sand*?"

Then she was gone, bounding down to the beach and east toward camp, with Stafford in pursuit, but before he could gain on her, she cut up from the water again and ran toward the dunes, tantalizingly slow at first, then in a burst of speed, disappearing over a low hill of sand before he had done much more than glimpse her starlit body.

Hell, she could cut her feet on some of the trash strung out along the upper beach or slash her legs on palmettos. Stafford struck out in the direction he had last seen her, keeping his eyes on the sand ahead, dodging cans and clumps of driftwood and whatever else seemed not to be sand, and as often as he dared he lifted his eyes to search for her. Her form flashed with dazzling speed across his line of vision between two dunes, rose as if by magic up the side of a farther mound of sand, then disappeared again.

"God . . . *damn*," he panted as he topped one of the dunes, "I am too fucking *old* for this." He dropped to his knees, his chest heaving, and tried to catch his breath.

"Jaaack."

He could see her just across a sandy flat at the foot of a taller dune, perhaps fifty feet away, her hands cupped to her mouth.

"Yooooooo, Jaaaack."

"Shit," he hissed and scrambled to his feet and lunged down the slope toward her. Before he was halfway to the spot where she'd been, she had crossed over the dune, almost twice as high as the one he had just descended from and, silhouetted against the night sky for a starlit instant, plunged into the dark again. His heart was hammering away under his ribs, his legs weak and watery and heavy as lead, but he hurled himself with lunatic frenzy against the steep hill of sand, sliding back two feet for every three he took in stride, trying to remember that he was the male in pursuit here. He fell forward onto his hands briefly, used them to steady himself, and, with one more heroic lunge in a flurry of sand, crested the peak and stood there humped over, gasping, while his pulse drummed away in his temples. Above him the stars stared coldly down.

"God*damn*," he whimpered, saliva stringing from his mouth. "Is this my Golgotha? All I need up here is a cross for her to nail me to." He dropped to his knees and slumped forward until his forehead touched the sand. In that position he rested.

"Hello, Pompeii Man."

He rose to his feet, hands on his knees, and squinted into the darkness before him. He wasn't sure where the voice had come from, only that it was close.

"Susie," he croaked.

"Right here, Pompeii Man."

He straightened. She was directly behind him, so close that he could feel her breath on the back of his neck. Her nipples touched him and the rest of her body closed on his as she wrapped her arms around his waist. The two stood in silence on the top of the dune, blended into one, then the wheezing man humped over again in dead knee-wobbling weariness, trying to recover his breath and focus his mind enough to think of what to make of the woman holding him.

"I've got sand all over me," he finally managed, straightening up again. "All over my—all over me."

"I've got it all over me too. Can't you feel it between us?"

He could. The tiny grains were all that separated him from the body he had craved for weeks now, and all he had to do was turn around and take her, sand and all, drive her hard against the dune until she screamed with pleasure, or *pain*—hell, at this point he didn't really care, wasn't sure there was a difference. But his penis was as useless as a piece of old greasy leather, coated with sand like a fish fillet in cornmeal, and he doubted that he had the strength to turn around and face her, much less summon the energy for love. He slumped forward again.

"Yes," he sighed, "I can feel the sand."

"Are you all right, Jack?" She was nuzzling the back of his neck.

"Yeah, yeah, I've got to get my breath back is all. I'm not used to chasing naked women in the dunes at night. Haven't done that in a while." He was still struggling for breath, but his heart was calming down. "Been at least a month."

She turned him around and molded her body against the front of his and kissed him strongly on the mouth. "My God, you've even got sand on your forehead."

"I know. All over me."

"I'm sorry, but it *was* fun, you know. And it was the first time for me too."

Strangely, though she had kissed him with passion, her breasts against his chest, his penis nestled in her sandy damp pubic hair, he felt nothing but gut-wrenching weariness.

In shape, shit, I'm as dead to my ass as an old man.

She backed away from him. "You want to go wash this sand off?"

"Yeah . . . uh . . . I guess so." He was taking deep breaths now, but he could barely stand.

He followed her back to the beach, trying to stay up on his trembling legs. *What a crazy-ass night.*

He watched her form move gracefully over the sand.

Out here with the most beautiful woman I've ever seen and I can't even get a hard-on when she touches me with a full frontal. His sandy penis swung from side to side as he walked.

In the water again, he felt his spirits recover a bit, though he was still weak in the legs as he waded out to where she scrubbed her body in the surf. Beside her he squatted and rubbed his hands over his arms and legs and torso, then ducked under and rinsed his hair and face. Last, he swished his penis around and carefully inspected it with his fingers to be certain that no grains of sand remained. If by some miracle he did manage to make it with her, he didn't want to ruin things with that damned sand.

"Is there any fresh water on the island where we can rinse?" she asked as she returned to the beach. "I think I've got all the sand off, but I don't know whether I can sleep with salt all over me."

He squatted down and rinsed one last time for good measure. "Well, there's an artesian well at the Ranger Station over on the inside beach, way over to the west, but we'd have a hell of a long walk over there in the dark and would probably get so sweaty and sandy that it wouldn't be worth it, not to mention the brush we'd have to get through. And mosquitoes. I have a five-gallon bucket of water in the boat. We can rinse off with that before we go to bed."

"There's my Pompeii Man again, thinking of everything."

"Yeah, well, your Pompeii Man is just about as dead as Pompeii itself right now."

She took his hand, and they walked up the beach toward camp, naked as newborns, though Stafford gave little thought to the fact as his body slowly returned to normal. He thought only of the walk over to the boat and the weight of a five-gallon bucket of water. He had hoped she would not mention the fact that they were still nude—as exhausted as he was, he wanted to see her naked in the light—but when they reached the spot where their things lay, she picked up her bathing suit and walked out into the surf and put it on, then her shirt, and he followed her lead, hating the feel of clothing against his nakedness. Perversely, only now, with his cutoffs back on, did he feel himself begin to stir.

The Coke they had when they got to camp almost fully revived Stafford's energy, and he shared a Butterfinger with Susie. At long last he felt like a man again, certainly strong enough to walk over to the boat and bring back the water, which in short order he did, returning to find her wrapped in a large towel and sitting between the tent and fire on one of the ice chests. His legs were still weak.

"I took my bathing suit off," she said, "so all I've got to do is rinse and dry off and slip on some clean clothes."

"You mean you don't have anything on under that towel?"

"Nothing. But why would that interest you? You had me up against you naked out there in the dunes and nothing happened."

"Susie, you—"

"I'm teasing, Jack, you know that. Come on and rinse me off."

She walked to the edge of their little circle of light and draped the towel over a bush. In the glow from the languishing fire her form was golden, so exquisitely perfect in every proportion: calves, thighs, buttocks, her back flaring into shoulders that, though broad and firm, seemed so astonishingly matched to the rest of her, and falling across them her hair, which even wet was a rich straw color.

"God," he breathed to himself, "this is the finest chapter in youth's sweet-scented manuscript."

"Ready?" She dropped her head back so that her hair fell free of her shoulders. "Just pour when you're ready."

Stafford twisted off the spout cap and hoisted the bucket to his shoulder, tilted it so that a steady stream of water came out instead of gulping chugs, and let the water wash down across her face and hair and shoulders as she turned to direct the stream where she wanted it to go. She was careful not to turn enough to the side that he could see her breasts. After he had emptied perhaps a third of the bucket, she said that she was rinsed well enough and reached for the towel and draped it around herself again.

"Do you want me to rinse *you?*" she asked when she had turned to face him.

"Well, that bucket's still pretty heavy. I'll just go off there in the dark and wash down. Won't take but a minute."

She handed him a towel, and Stafford lugged the bucket around one of the dunes and, after draping the towel across a shrub, lifted the bucket, allowing the water to cascade down over his head and shoulders and torso; then he splashed off his legs and carefully rinsed his penis. He dried himself off in the dark and carried what remained of the water back to camp.

Susie was dressed in a pair of clean shorts and tee-shirt when he set the bucket down beside the tent.

He squinted. "What does your tee-shirt say?"

She laughed. "SQUEEZE ME."

"That an invitation?"

"Could be."

He set the bucket down beside the tent. "Well, listen, there's enough water left for us to rinse down again, if we decide to take another swim."

"That what you want to do? Swim?" She was combing out her hair, wincing as she encountered knots.

"No, no," he said. "Just that *if* we decide to swim, we have water to rinse off again."

"What I'd really like to do, after you get some clothes on, is walk on the beach again, look at the stars awhile. Would you like to do that with me, Pompeii Man?"

"Absolutely. Give me a second."

Stafford rummaged around in the picnic basket until he found a small paper sack wrapped with a piece of twine, untied it, and pulled out a tee-shirt, some jockey shorts, and another pair of cut-offs.

"My, but you travel light," she observed as he pushed back the flaps of the tent and pulled himself up inside, cantilevering his legs outside through the flaps and rubbing his feet together to clean them of sand. He pivoted on his butt, swung his legs into the tent, removed the towel, and pulled on his clean dry clothes.

"Ready," he grunted as he crawled out and spread the towel over the top of the tent, where she had already draped hers.

They walked west along the beach, noting the scattered lights at sea. He pointed out constellations to her, identifying some individual stars, and remarked that if they stood still for a bit they might see a satellite zipping along. So they stood then, still as the night itself, with him right behind her, pressing his body to hers, taking care not to touch her with his hardness.

In a few minutes, as he had predicted, something that to the casual eye might escape attention moved from north to south across the starry sky, appearing at times to feint and dodge.

He brought his right arm up and pointed, leaning his head in against hers.

"There. There's one."

She watched for a few seconds where he pointed, then nodded.

"Yes, yes, I see it, like a moving star."

"Right, just like a moving star. And if we stayed here watching long enough, we'd see five, maybe ten, of them tonight. It's amazing how many are out there."

He had kept his face pressed against hers, his chin on her shoulder. She seemed to be pressing back.

"Susie, may I kiss you?"

For an answer she turned and put an arm around his neck, pulling his lips down to hers, and this time he knew that she was feeling something, something strong, and he turned so that his hardness was against her.

"Enough, Jack," she said after a brief while. She pulled away from him. "The ground rules go for both of us." She dropped her right hand and formed it around the bulge. "There'll be another time for him. And her. They'll get together, sooner or later. As much as they'd like to tonight, we can't let it happen."

"Susie."

She lifted her hand and held it over his mouth. "No, Jack, not tonight. A lot rides on what happens tonight. If you let me control this . . . if you just leave me in charge of this part of it. Well, we'll both in time be glad, that's all."

Goddamn, he breathed to himself, *how I would like to be back on that dune top right now and you naked and against me.* He had never in his whole life been so turned on, so on the very edge of exploding. Was she on her period, or what? *You will be serviced tonight, my man, if it has to be done with the old right hand.*

Back at camp, he let her crawl into the tent and spread the blankets to suit herself. There would be one beneath them and one to cover them, with a third folded and laid across the open end of the tent to serve as a pillow. Once they were in for the evening he would zip up the mosquito flaps and nothing would pester them.

"Ready, I guess," she said, poking her head out. "I need to brush my teeth and make a little bathroom trip, and then we can turn in, if you want. It must be getting late."

Stafford, building up the fire for the night, shrugged. "Dunno. I didn't bring a watch." He looked up toward the stars, as if they would tell him anything. "I'd guess around nine or ten."

"Well," she said, standing up and stretching, "we're on Pompeii time, so it doesn't matter."

He went behind one of the dunes while she made her trip in the opposite direction. When she came back to the fire, he was through brushing his teeth and standing there shirtless, wondering whether he should remove his cutoffs.

"You ready to go to bed?" she asked, shaking out her hair, which had now dried to its lighter natural shade.

"Guess so. You?"

"Do you sleep naked, Jack?" she asked.

"No. Undershorts. You?"

"Panties and a tee-shirt usually. I'm not sure out here. Should I wear bullhides?"

Stafford laughed. "Hey, I told you, you're in control here. I'll do whatever you let me do. If you'll sleep naked, that's the way I want it. I will too."

"Tee-shirt and panties, and you keep your shorts on."

"Yes'm."

"Really, Jack."

"Really," he said.

When the two of them were inside, Stafford zipped up the mosquito netting at the opening and they stretched out, facing the sea. The tent was pretty tight with two occupants, though he had spent several nights in it with a woman in Colorado— most of the time they had not been side-by-side. The evening was still fairly warm, so he suggested that they fold the top blanket back at their feet and pull it up if they needed it, as they probably would along toward morning, when the wind would switch and the late September sea breeze would have a bite to it.

They lay for a long while on their stomachs watching faraway lights move across the Gulf and talking freely about themselves, something they had not done much on their earlier dates. He learned that she was an only child of divorced parents and that her mother lived in Mobile, where she ran a small antique store just off Government Boulevard and lived comfortably enough off the trickle of income from the store and the beneficence of her husband, an attorney, who felt an obligation to maintain Susie and her mother in some style. Susie had chosen the community college in Gautier because she wanted to live somewhere other than the city her mother lived in and because she wanted to be near the Coast.

Stafford told her a bit about his childhood and education and travels, finally working the divorce into the conversation, though she seemed to have no reaction at all to it except to observe when he had finished talking about his former wife that he seemed to have had a fairly eventful life.

"You're a man of the world, Jack Stafford. You have been everywhere and done everything. I've never known a man who had any depth at all." She laughed. "Really, I've known nothing but boys."

"The world's a big place, Susie, and I haven't seen a sliver of it. Not nearly as much as I want to see."

"I haven't seen *any* of it," she said quietly.

He reached and placed his hand on her head and stroked her hair. "Maybe I can change that someday."

"I'm still kind of warm," she said. "I don't suppose you'd mind if I took off this tee-shirt?"

He laughed. "Let me think about it."

"These blankets aren't exactly as comfortable as sheets."

Remaining on her stomach, she twisted and tugged until the tee-shirt was off. She tucked it into a corner of the tent.

The wind, he noticed, had swung around to the north, occasionally gusting and flinging sand against the foot of the tent, another reason he had chosen to face it seaward. She lay now with her hands still beneath her chin, looking out toward the Gulf, but she was speaking less frequently and more slowly.

"I guess it would be in keeping with the ground rules, wouldn't it, if I kissed you good-night?" He ran his hand lightly across her shoulders.

She tilted her face to him and said, "Yes, I guess it would."

She kissed him without passion on the lips and lowered her head to the pillow blanket, her face turned away from him. For a long time he lay propped up on an elbow gazing down on the beautiful woman stretched out beside him, even in starlight amazingly perfect in proportion. Her hair was swept back toward Stafford, trailing out to his end of the rolled blanket, and when he laid his face down, he touched the hair, and all the mingled smells of Susie Clayburn and the beach came through his nostrils and mouth and he had to fight the urge to roll over and take care of things for himself in a few easy strokes. In a while, lulled by her soft, even breathing, a kind of peace settled over him and he flattened out and slept, his face nuzzling her hair.

He awoke deep in the night. They were still lying on their stomachs, uncovered, their thighs touching. Dark as it was inside the tent, he could see that she was resting her chin on the rolled up blanket with her eyes wide open.

"You awake?" he asked softly.

"Yes. There's lightning off there." She pointed to the southeast. "It's running everywhere, great long streaks."

But there was no thunder coming across the water to them, so he assured her that it was probably just heat lightning and nothing to worry about.

"Besides, we're in a tent."

"It's awfully delicate," she whispered, turning over, her arm falling across the small of his back.

"Believe me, it'll take a beating. I've been through several storms in this little orange tent, and it'll keep us dry."

He dared not look directly at her, but he could see in the corner of his eye her breasts and her panties.

"I wonder what time it is." Her fingers were delicately stroking the lower part of his back.

"Dunno," Stafford answered. "It's got to be somewhere in the early morning. Maybe around two or three. Should have brought a watch."

Hell, he didn't have any idea at all what time it was. And he didn't care. He was trying to figure out what her hand on his back meant.

"Hasn't cooled off a whole lot yet, has it?" she asked.

He turned his face to hers. "Well, it's cooler than it was."

"When I woke up, my hair was all over your face."

"I know," Stafford said, rising on an elbow, his mouth only inches from hers. "It smells like the sea. I went to sleep smelling it. It was wonderful. It's the color of Smithers' sea oats, you know. Exactly the color of the sea oats. Every time I think of you, I think of the sea, of the islands. And it'll be even worse from now on."

"Why's that?"

"Because every time I'm out here, I'll think of this night, of you, of our lying here side by side. I'll think of swimming naked with you, chasing you naked in the dunes."

"Maybe I'll be with you," she said softly. "Then you won't have to think about tonight."

He leaned and kissed her softly and she dropped her head back down on the blanket, arms spread. Her breasts were clearly visible to him in starlight from the tent opening. They were small, but absolutely perfect in shape. He rose to his knees and kissed the lobe of her ear, moved slowly to her neck, then shoulder, on to the inside of the arm that lay on his side of the blanket, inching along until his tongue touched her finger tips. He could feel tiny goose bumps springing up as his tongue moved.

She said nothing when he shifted his lips across to her left breast, where his tongue sought out and circled her nipple, and still said nothing when he delicately tongued the other nipple and eased his mouth toward her navel, where he tasted salt. He did not want to rush, to feverishly set upon her the way he knew any boys she'd had so far had probably done, making her defensive and nervous. His older women had taught him how to love slowly and methodically, savoring every inch of the body. As he moved lower, she moaned, and by the time he had gone past her navel and run his tongue along the top of her panties, he could feel a vague motion in her hips.

He worked down the inside of her thigh to her knee, shifted to the other thigh, and moved back up, all the while spreading her legs wider until by the time he had reached the spot, she was open to him, the only thing separating him from her the thin panties, through which he could already feel her wetness.

"Susie," he leaned and whispered in her ear.

Still she said nothing. The only sound was the swishing of the water before them.

To his mild surprise he felt no urgency, only the slow realization that it was going to happen, that this woman was allowing him to do what she had already said that they would not do, that they were one with the night and the sea and consummation was near. He slipped her panties down and off, folded them carefully, and laid them in the corner of the tent.

"Unless you tell me not to, I've got to go out there and get something. Be right back."

When still she did not speak, he crawled out of the tent and went to the picnic basket and removed his wallet, where he had stashed it earlier, and fished out a condom and crawled back in the tent. She was still on her back with her legs spread.

"I figured you had that base covered."

He slipped off his shorts and removed the condom from its package. "You never know. Everything but tongs."

He dropped between her legs and began kissing her breasts as he probed until he slid effortlessly inside her and she took him completely.

And then there was only that timeless void, which a man and woman know when their passion has risen past all reasonable restraint, that instant when the earth stands still on its axis or spins wildly out of control, when reality is just that man and that woman, wherever they happen to be.

When the sun found them that Sunday morning, lightening up the little orange tent, Jack Stafford was still intertwined with Susie Clayburn, while before them the great Gulf rolled in and rushed up the sand, remembered itself, and drew back again.

FROM CHAPTER XIX

Now they were on Horn Island, mid-afternoon on a Friday, this the first day of what he planned to be a full weekend trip out. It was something that he proposed and she had, to his great surprise, agreed to. It was not exactly agreement—she simply did not object. She said that since she had nothing else to do she would go. It was something to do. At least no one would see them on the island.

He borrowed Jerry Harmon's small power-boat and met her at the old Coast Guard station near the mouth of the Pascagoula. She sat in the car until he tied up at the dock and walked over and opened the door for her.

"Ready?" he asked.

"I guess so."

She looked around to see whether she recognized anyone who might know her.

"Do you have everything in the boat?"

"Everything except your bag." He pointed at the blue overnighter she had brought with her.

She reached and got the bag and her drawing equipment, which she had wedged behind the seat.

"You're going to paint, I see," he said.

"Maybe. Depends."

She clamped a white beach hat on her head and adjusted her sunshades. She wore a white jumpsuit, and a thin white scarf curled around her neck and rose to the chin. She was white from head to foot

"People are going to wonder who I'm taking to sea," he said playfully to her as he escorted her across the shell parking lot.

"Let'm wonder," she said.

She walked in silence beside him and allowed him to help her into the boat. She took a seat forward and stared straight ahead as he eased the boat out of the estuary and into the Gulf.

He crouched in their old camping spot, the ice chest and rolled-up tent and sacks of provisions surrounding him like a man who has circled wagons for the night to guard against whatever threat might be arrayed in the dunes or in the trees beyond.

Between him and the beach, just outside the circle, Susie sat, her legs drawn up tight to her chest, eyes fixed on the vast Gulf that stretched out before her. When they reached the camp site, she had taken off her scarf and hat and jumpsuit, beneath which she wore a pair of cut-off jeans and an old denim shirt. On the back of the shirt at some point in the past she had drawn in acrylics a clump of sea oats. Now her hair fell across the oats and blended with them so that Stafford could not tell one from the other.

There was no sign of the marker they had left. In a way he was glad—one of the last things he wanted to see again was a cross. He felt so dreadfully alone, as if a universe of cold stars separated them and not just a few feet of still-warm sand.

He rose and walked down to her. "I'm glad you came," he said as the surf rolled in and swished and rolled back out again.

"Me too." She pulled her legs beneath her on the sand. "It's good to be away from the house, and we couldn't have chosen better weather."

With quickened pulse he reached and took her hand, though he did not look at her, nor she at him. She did not try to pull her hand away. In the corner of his eye he could see her hair loose in the breeze and brilliantly blond in the late sun, which was at least two hours from touching the Gulf to the west.

Faint bruises still ran along her upper arm, but they were fading like distant rained-out storm clouds, yellowish-purple and vague, and her face had recovered its youthful perfection. It was all he could do to keep from pulling her to him, but he knew that patience was the key now, a slow, careful reknitting of the fabric that had been torn. This would be the night, he hoped, when they could renew their faith and come together as they had that other night in this spot, when they blended their bodies for the first time.

"Do you want to walk down the beach?" he asked her. "We can set up the tent later. I'll light the Coleman if I have to."

She stood and brushed the sand off her legs.

"Just leave everything like it is, Jack. I'm not sure I want to spend the night out here. Let me think about it. I would like to go and sketch some. You come and get me later, before dark." She said it in a tone that allowed for no argument.

"Would you like to swim first? It's not too cool."

"Not really," she said.

"So where'll I find you?"

"Over there." She pointed down the beach toward the falling sun. "In the dunes. Follow my tracks. You'll find me."

He shrugged. "If that's what you want."

"Yes."

She walked up past him and removed her sketchpad and handful of chalks from one of the bags. She slipped the pieces of chalk in her shirt pocket and clamped the pad under her arm.

"I'll be along to get you in a couple of hours," he said. "I think I'll cast a little."

She did not answer. He watched her walk slowly toward the surf, then west, still with a slight limp, keeping just at the edge of the water.

God, God, will it ever come right again?

He sat on the ice chest and had a beer, then walked down to the surf, and cast awhile, working up and down the beach from the campsite. The sun fell relentlessly toward the water, squatting finally, an angry ball of molten fire that seemed to intensify as it sank, then sliding perceptibly into a sea that seemed to dissolve the fire and spread it across the whole horizon. Halfway expecting to hear it hiss out, he was amazed at how quickly it dropped until nothing but afterglow remained.

"It sank right on New Orleans," he said to the red sky. "May God damn New Orleans. May it burn like hell itself."

He carried his rod back up to the campsite, opened another beer, and drank it as he walked along the tideline, following the tracks his wife had made, the sand lit by the glow of the sky stretched out like one vast smear of blood.

In the afterglow of the red western sky he followed her tracks just outside the slick sand of the tidal beach, now simply a damp mantle dotted with fresh shells left by the falling water, and at length he found her. She had very deliberately kept just inside the white sand above the tideline, like a child afraid of water, and he could see where here and there she had stepped up on the shelf where the water could not reach, but as far as he could tell she had not paused anywhere to look at anything, to study gnarled driftwood or a shell. She had kept to her purpose, walking westward on the beach toward the falling sun, which sank somewhere beyond that eyeball of water that stared off into space.

She sat on top of the dune where she had sat that day that seemed now so very long ago, her back to him, and for an instant he fancied that nothing had changed, that she was the girl she had been, when with her sketchpad she had recorded in chalk pastels what she saw in the sky and trees and soft stretch of island in front of her, that day when her sketch showed green trees and palmettos and pelicans, which she thought were gulls, flying across a pale blue sky with puffy little clouds like ghosts.

She was twisted down in an uncomfortable-looking hunch, legs folded under, the sketchpad on the sand beside her, staring out toward the distant line of trees, or beyond. A lone storm cloud skirted the coast, nearing the shipyard, whose lights were now blazing bright across the darkening water. All along the shore, lights stretched out as far as he could see.

He climbed the dune and eased down beside her. "I didn't know you had come so far."

She turned and looked at him or past him into the red smear where the sun had been. Her face was expressionless, as if it held nothing for him, as if it were merely there like anything else that had washed up on the beach and tumbled in the wind to lodge on the high dune. He wasn't even sure that she could focus on him anymore.

"I thought you were coming sooner. I have decided that I want to go back tonight."

"But all the stuff—"

"I never did agree to spend the night out here, Jack. You reached that conclusion on your own. I want to go back. I'll help you load the boat."

"It'll be way after dark by the time we get in the river. Those crabtrap markers are going to be hard to spot."

"You can do it. You've done it before. I can hold a light."

"OK. If that's the way you want it."

He pointed at the sketchpad. "Have you drawn anything?"

She nodded and held it out to him.

He kneeled before her and accepted it and lifted the heavy cardboard lid, turning it under. But there was only a blank page.

She reached and flipped the page and in the twilight a panorama of savage color leapt at him. She gripped the corner of the pad and twisted it until it was horizontal on his lap. Then he saw shapes rise out of surrealistic slashes of red and orange, black and green. This time the sky was the color of a bruise, and towering clouds with anvils swirling out from their tops trundled across it. Beneath the ominous sky the trees were stark, their arms flung out, with here and there an osprey nest wedged in their crotches, pale chrysalises with cruelly curved beaks thrust out of them, like some hellish scene out of Breughel or Bosche, but what caught his eye much more than the sky and the trees was the thick spiral of vultures at whose base an animal lay splayed, a confusion of red and black, unidentifiable organs strung out on the sand, its visage grotesquely twisted by pain as if the animal still felt the fierce, lacerating beaks of birds. And in the foreground, as if deliberately placed there by some villainous child, the beach was clotted with cans and jars, lumps of tar, snarls of rope, and rusty wire mesh. Horrid shapes of driftwood, like sun-bleached bones of the shattered dead, jutted from the sand.

He shook his head. "You drew this?"

"Yes."

"You did all this this afternoon?"

"It's not finished," she said. "I've been working on it for days. It's one reason I wanted to come back out here. To get the colors right."

Stafford looked out toward the trees.

"I don't see these colors, these shapes. There are no buzzards out there. I've never seen your sketches with so much color, and with such violence. I didn't even know they made chalks with colors as sharp as these."

She shrugged and stared off away from him.

"I don't understand, Susie. What's all this about? You haven't sketched what's out here. This isn't you."

"You don't know what's me and what isn't, Jack. Not anymore. And you don't know *what* I see." She was looking toward the line of dark trees. "And I'm not sure I do either. I sketched what my mind saw, and it was like something or someone was guiding my hand."

She pointed to the drawing. "It was almost like I didn't have any control over what my hand drew there. I am so damned *confused.*"

"Susie," he tried.

"Jack, listen to me." She had reached and clutched his arm with a grip of surprising strength.

"What? What, Susie? Talk to me."

"I didn't tell you everything he said." She still was not looking at him.

"Everything *who* said?"

He held the pad out to her, and she loosened her grip on his arm and took it.

"The man."

"What man, Susie?"

"*The* man, Jack. Satan."

Stafford leaned toward her and placed his hand on her shoulder, but she withdrew from his touch. "What else did the sonofabitch say?"

"He told me, Jack."

Stafford held his breath and looked at her. "Told you what? *What* did he tell you?"

"He told me—he told me why they took me." Then she turned to face him.

Stafford stared at her eyes, in which he could see a reflection of the red evening.

"He told me, Jack. He told me what you told that bartender. And, by the way, *he* was the *white* guy who raped me, the bartender. I remembered his rings. And those ghastly hairy arms."

"But, Susie, you said—"

"I guess I didn't want to believe it at first. And then, once I did start believing it . . . I mean, how could he have made that up, or *why* would he? Once I did start believing it, I wasn't certain I wanted to hurt you." She held the pad in her lap. "Not that you didn't deserve being hurt."

"But now you've decided to?"

"I decided that if we are ever going to get on with our lives, I've got to tell you everything."

"Susie, I just don't know what to say to you."

"And he told me that it didn't matter who I was or who I belong to, that if I wanted to be with him I could be. He'll take me. No matter who I am. Any time I want to go."

She turned her face back toward the trees. "Jack, I'm not sure who I belong with anymore. He was so gentle. . . ."

"Susie, he—*they* raped you, brutalized you." He clenched his eyes and still he saw her face against the sky, the image reversed, the sky dark, her face and hair a ghostly white.

"My life is a ruin, Jack, hollow and senseless, and I can't get a focus on it anymore. I don't know who to trust, who to turn to. It's like my head has been emptied out and filled up with things I never knew before. It's like I've seen through to the other side of something but I can't make out the shapes. I am afraid of my own shadow."

She closed the sketchpad and scooped up her things. "Come on, now. I want to go back."

Stafford watched as his wife descended the dune and walked toward the slick tideline. His eyes swept the darkening landscape once more and settled on the red-gold spread of sun-emblazened sky beyond the great unblinking eyeball of water that stared off into nothing. Now Jack Stafford understood about Pompeii and China and Greece and the immense energy of the sun, the boiling fountains of light of the stars, the cold barren loneliness of timeless space, and man's ridiculous folly and puny, tragic insignificance in it all, a creature that found substance and meaning and value only through the wild dreams he conjured up in his haunted head.

As he knelt there on the hill of sand, watching in the afterglow of the western sky the shadows of evening settle on the island like black ashes, or merely like dust or sand, swallowing everything into a suffocating wordless dark, Jack Stafford finally understood.

Cleo

M any a year Clyde McManus stood and watched a ship he had had a hand in building slide down the ramp at the little shipyard he worked at in Pascagoula, splash into saltwater for the first time, rock gently, steady itself, and then move smoothly out to the Gulf for a trial run and then to wherever it was headed. He watched until it became a mere speck on its way to the pass between Petit Bois and Horn and nodded his head with both satisfaction and sadness—satisfaction that with his own hands he had once again helped build something so magnificent, so sleek and graceful, sadness in knowing that, as he might have to give up a beautiful woman, he had to let her go.

When finally it came time for him to retire, he tallied eighty-three boats and ships, wooden-hulled and steel, he had helped build, eighty-three launches of those beautiful ladies he so lovingly touched and then watched glide away. Most he never saw again.

The morning he walked away from the shipyard for the last time, he ran his hand along the smooth side of a shrimper being readied for launch the following Sunday. He thought about going back to see her glide off to the south, but decided against it. He looked about to make certain no one was looking, then leaned and kissed the white-painted steel hull and left.

It was the Fourth of July, and they were crowded around the plate-glass doors leading to the patio in the little Mississippi coastal house the children had grown up in, and now they stood in silent awe watching their father work. There were the two sons, the daughter, their spouses, and seven grandchildren. It was the first time they had all been together in nearly ten years, time having scattered them across the country. And the reason they finally all came home was what was sitting in the backyard of their parents' home. When word came of it, there was no way not to come—this was serious family business.

John Turner was the oldest of the children and generally tried to take charge in such issues. He liked for people to use both his first and middle name, since his father's first name was John too, though he went by Clyde. Finally he turned from the glass sliding doors that looked out onto the yard and spoke to Cora, his mother, who was hard at work in the kitchen and staying out of the mess the best she could.

"Momma, what possessed him to start this?"

"At's his binness, John Turner. We discussed it, but I left the decision up to him. It keeps him busy, at least. And happy. Lots of men can't handle retirement and just stay under the women's feet, lay on the couch and watch the TV or drink theirselves to death, so I figure I got lots to be glad about." She pushed the kitchen curtain aside and watched her husband a few seconds, then let the curtain fall back.

"Momma." The daughter spoke from the sliding door. Her voice had an urgent edge to it. "Why is it so *big*? Marvin says it looks to be more than thirty feet long."

Cora stirred her peas. "Exactly forty-two feet, not counting the figurehead."

"Forty-two feet?" The others turned their faces toward the kitchen, then back to the yard.

It was like they were watching something in an aquarium, with the children pressing their faces to the glass, the boat a derelict lying in the sand and gravel and any second a big fish would come swimming by.

"The figurehead will add another four feet. It's the head and bosom of an African queen. He got it—"

"Forty-two feet." John Turner squinted out at the scaffolding, where Clyde was wrestling with a piece of timber. "That's a hell of a lot of boat."

Cora continued: "You better not call it a boat in front of him. To him, and to me, it is a ship. He got the figurehead from a sailor that brought it back from some little town on the coast of Africa."

"And let me guess," the daughter said, walking into the kitchen and lifting the lid off the rice, something she always did, much to Cora's irritation, "he's going to call the boat the *African Queen*, right?"

Cora shook her head. "Nope. Gon' call her *Cleo*, short for *Cleopatra*—she was a African queen. And it is a ship, not a boat."

The daughter snorted. "*Cleo*? Well, that is a dumb name for a boat, if you ask me," she said. "That sounds like a name of a colored girl that comes by to clean your house."

"Nobody ast you," Cora replied. "That's her name. And it's a *ship*, not a damn boat."

"It looks like to me," John Turner said, "that he could use some help with them timbers. How come he won't let us help him out?"

Cora, her head half in the maw of the oven, echoed back, "He won't let nobody help him but me, and he won't even let me come out there without it's something he knows full well he can't do on his own. Y'all know your daddy." She closed the oven door. "Or at least you used to."

She straightened up and brushed her apron front. "He had to call Floyd Robinson over last week to help him get part of some new scaffolding up, since we tried and tried and couldn't do it by ourselves. It liked to have killed him to call Floyd over, much as he's helped him with stuff over the years."

Her face grew stern.

"John Turner, don't y'all dare go out there. He'll just yell at you and be in a bad mood the rest of the day and set to drinkin'.

This is something he's bound and determined to do on his own. And if I was y'all, I'd get away from them doors before he throws a hammer at you. You look like a bunch of fools with your faces pressed to that glass."

John Turner muttered something to the others about "looking at a fool," and they all moved back to the living room.

The very day of his retirement from Crump Shipbuilding, Clyde had called Cora out to his shop, where blueprints for a large vessel lay unrolled and taped together in four sections on a work table. In one corner was a profile sketch of the completed craft, its sails full of wind and two figures, a man and woman, sitting in deck chairs on the bow. He pointed to the sketch.

"Sam Buckley drawed the pitcher for me. What do you think?"

"Sam has drawed up enough boats that he ought to be able to do one right. Looks right nice."

"I am not asking how you like Sam's drawing. How do you like the ship? It is a ship, not a boat. It's a modified ketch. Diesel powered with optional sails, over forty feet long, can go anywhere in the world. Sam drawed it up from some old plans he found in the shop."

Cora studied the plans a while, the way she would go over a recipe. "It's a nice boat, Clyde. *Ship.* But what are you doing with these plans? You ain't forgot already that you've retired?" She leaned forward and looked over the plans again.

"It's *our* ship, Cora, mine and yours. These are the plans for *Cleo*, which is what we are gon' call her, short for *Cleopatra.*" He put his battered right index finger on the couple in the deck chairs. "That's us."

Then he pointed to the figurehead, an ebony face and shoulders with a ribbon of red cloth covering the breasts. "I got a sailor getting me one of these from Nigerier. Hand-carved. It's the real thing. Got a real nigger carving it out of a solid log. Teak or mahogany. Something like that."

Cora stood a long time looking at the sketch in the corner. "Somehow this is not what I figured you were going to do when you retired."

"You gotta dream big, girl. The world's our oysture now. A few months, and I'll do what I been doing for most of my life: I'm gon' build us a ship."

When she walked back into the house, she wasn't sure exactly what she was supposed to be thinking.

Nothing more was said about the *Cleo* until a few days later, when, just before noon on a Saturday, three heavily loaded flat-bed trucks pulled up to the curb out front. Cora stood behind the den drapes, her hand to her mouth, and watched as each truck backed in and unloaded. In a frenzy of excitement Clyde dashed back and forth directing the unloading. When the trucks left, the corner of the lot that she had intended to be filled with rows of vegetables the next spring, now that Clyde had time to garden seriously, was covered with stacks of timbers.

Clyde was sitting on a mountain of beams figuring with a pencil when Cora walked out. "When you said you was building a boat, a ship, I really thought you meant some kind of big model, like for the mantle, three or four feet long." She stared at the piles of lumber. "But them stacks of lumber tells me I was wrong."

He stopped scribbling. "I told you it was a ship, a real ship. Forty-two feet long."

"Clyde, you can't build a ship that big in the backyard. You ain't got a permit from the city. Who will you get to help you? Who'll buy it? How would you get it moved?"

"The hell with the city. I ain't read nowhere in the laws that a man can't build a ship in his backyard if he wants to. I bet you a dollar to a dog's ass that there ain't a rule wrote down nowhere that says a man can't build a ship in his yard. And I ain't going to sell it. I told you it's going to be *ours*."

"Clyde, we ain't ever owned even a skiff. What would we do with a boat forty feet long?"

"Forty-*two*," he said, sliding down off the timbers and disappearing into the shop. "And it is a Goddamn *ship*."

That evening, after she had washed the supper dishes, Cora walked out into the dark yard, where she could vaguely see Clyde, crouched on a stack of beams, silhouetted against the sky. He looked like some kind of big sea bird that had come in for the evening to roost.

"I don't guess I have to ast what you're thinking about." She rested her chin beside one of his feet.

"No, I reckon not. You want to come up here?"

In answer she raised her arms to him, and he helped her onto the stack. They sat dangling their legs off, the way she remembered doing when they were first married, when all Clyde wanted to do on his time off was sit at the boat dock watching the bright boats, all sizes, shapes, and colors, go out into the Gulf. They would sit for hours with their legs dangling off the pier, sometimes talking quietly, sometimes just watching in silence as ripples from the boats washed across their feet. "Someday," Clyde would say, looking out toward the Gulf, "I am going to have a boat of my own."

"I don't suppose," he broke into her reverie, "that this makes much sense to you."

"More than you think."

"It's just that, well, all my grown-up life I have worked at building boats and ships for other people: shrimpers, tugs, yachts, small freighters, fishing boats, and I have watched them one by one head off from the shipyard dock to places I've just dreamed about going. Oh, some of them are still right here in Pascagoula, but at least they get out into the Gulf. Do you realize, Cora, that I have never even touched the saltwater outside the islands except when I was fishin' in the surf at Petit Bois or Horn?"

She patted his arm.

"Never been much out of the mouth of the river. Guys I've worked with for forty years have talked about fishing in the deep waters off Petit Bois and Horn Island, but I've never even been out there. Never been out of the Sound. And people having the ships built coming in and talking about all the places they were going to go in them. Jesus Christ, Cora, I've never been anywhere."

He pointed out toward the sky above the Gulf. "Even during the war, when other people got shipped off to Yerp or the South Pacific, I rode on a Goddamned train to Fort McClellan, Alabama, and I stayed at Fort McClellan the whole two and a half years during the war. The only fightin' I seen was in a bar. I wanted to be in the Navy. That's what I wanted. But it never worked out."

"So you're going to try to do now what you wanted to do all along?"

"Yeah. I got the time now, we got the money and this won't cost as much as you think, me doing all the building, and there's all them boxes of stainless steel screws and bolts and brass fittings in the shop, which I ain't been stealin' all these years for nothing."

"You *stole* all that stuff? You told me you got it at the salvage yard."

"Well, I lied. I got some of it from salvage, but I stole most of it. But the statue of lamentations has run out on it now, so they can't persecute me."

"You *stole* all that stuff! That ain't like you."

"Most of it would of been wasted anyhow, Cora. You wouldn't believe what them people thowe away."

She laughed. "I guess I ort to be mad at you, but now I just think it's funny. If you'd worked a few years longer, you could of stole a whole ship. Kinda like that Johnny Cash song, where he steals all them car parts and puts together a Cadillac."

"Might near could," he said. "Might near."

They were quiet for a few minutes.

"I got the know-how. Cora, Honey, this is our one chance to break out, to . . . you understand."

"I wondered. . . ."

He pulled her close to him.

"We have always had something come between us and what I think we've both wanted to do. I mean, admit it, Cora, you've wanted to break away and leave all this behind us, ain't you? Kids and yards and cooking and keeping house?"

"Well, I don't know about—"

"Ain't you ever thought about being out on the sea, free, the wind in your face, going places, seeing things we've never seen before? Cora, think how few times we have been out of Missippi. None, except for trips to Atlanter and Birminham to visit family. We ain't never been anywhere because we just wanted to go there."

"Not really. There was that one time we take'n the kids and drove over to AstroWorld in Houston. That's all."

"Hell, girl, think about all the countries out there we could visit by sea. Just think of it! A ship the size this one's gon' be will be able to go just about anywhere."

And think of it she did as *Cleo* rose from the backyard like something coming up out of the earth itself. She found herself more and more drawn to the smudged and dog-eared volumes in the bookcase beside their bed: *Robinson Crusoe*, *Mutiny on the Bounty*, *Two Years Before the Mast*, books on sailing and ships and navigation, maps of the world's seas, magical dreamlands that Clyde had lost himself in all those years when work and the kids and subsistence income had kept him landlocked, had not even allowed him into the waters of the deeper Gulf, which he could see from the seat of a crane at Crump's.

After that July the 4th, when the kids first saw the beginnings of the *Cleo*, there were persistent phone calls and letters asking about the project.

"Oh, it's coming right along," Cora would answer. "Your daddy's not the fastest shipbuilder in the world, but he's real good at it. He's doin' it right is whut."

One evening while Clyde was stretched out on the couch after a particularly exhausting day of beam wrestling, the phone rang and Cora answered. It was the daughter.

"Oh, it's coming along all right," he heard Cora say. "You know how your daddy works—slow but sure." After a few seconds she lowered her voice. "Now Ruth Ann, y'all don't worry about what he's spending."

"You tell her," Clyde yelled down the hallway, "that I am going to spend ever red-ass cent I got saved on that ship and when I die at the wheel somewhere off the coast of India or Africa, they can pack up and come help you sail'r home! Then it'll be up to you to decide how to satisfy'm."

Cora laughed when she came back to the den. "Lord, Clyde, she heard you."

"Good." After that there were fewer letters and phone calls inquiring about the *Cleo*.

Over the weeks the bottom beam fleshened into bright ribs. Then came heavy planks, which Clyde sometimes had to steam over washpots to get the wood to bend and fit properly, and caulking shone like veins along the deep sweep of the sides.

Neighbors leaned over fences and talked and pointed, cars drove slowly past, and sometimes people would stop and stare from the street. One afternoon two little boys ran and hoisted themselves onto the wooden fence surrounding the yard and clung with their chins on their hands shouting, "Noah, Noah!" until Clyde crawled over the edge of the boat and threw a hammer toward them.

One Sunday, just as Clyde and Cora were sitting down for a noon meal of fried chicken and creamed potatoes and gravy and all the other things that go well with them, John Turner and his wife and children dropped in.

"What brings y'all by?" Clyde asked, poised over a drumstick.

John Turner was holding back the den curtains. "Just wanted to see how your boat's coming. We were driving over to Mobile to hear the Blackwood Brothers. Thought we'd drop by."

"Real sweet of you, Son," Cora answered. "It does a heart good to see your folks and then go listen to gospel music."

Clyde had continued with his chicken, but he paused long enough to say, "It is a *ship*."

"We don't get over this way much, New Orleans being so far away," John Turner's wife said.

Clyde wiped his mouth on the sleeve of his khaki workshirt. "We noticed. At least a hour and a half." He rose from the table and reached for his hat. "Well, I got to get back at it. Y'all enjoy your visit."

"Daddy." John Turner cleared his throat. "Could we talk a few minutes?"

Clyde hung his hat back. "If it can be quick. I got lots to do today." He sat down beside Cora on the couch, but she got up and went into the kitchen.

"You boys go on outside," John Turner told his sons. "Ruby, you go read something in the bedroom." The little girl started down the hall, and the boys walked toward the back door.

"Naw, not out back," Clyde said, pointing toward the front door. "Go out that way. Y'all stay out of the backyard."

"But we want to see the boat," one of them whined.

"It is a Goddamned *ship*. Just stay away from the *Cleo*. Go out front. Play in the traffic."

"Daddy!" John Turner started.

"Clyde," Cora cautioned from the kitchen, "try not to talk that way around the kids."

"Then somebody ort to teach 'm the difference between a boat and a ship."

When the children were gone, John Turner and his wife sat down on either side of the old couple.

"Now, Daddy," he began, laying his hand on Clyde's knee, "I am representing the family here today—they have elected me their spokesman."

"The family, huh?" Clyde shook his head and lifted his son's hand off his knee and dropped it like a piece of concrete. "Since when did the family not include me and your momma? Or are you in on this too, Cora?"

"I got nothing to do with it, Clyde. I don't know nothing about what John Turner's talking about."

"So the family, whoever that is, elected you spokesman, boy?"

"Yessir," said John Turner, looking over at his wife, who, it was apparent, had just as soon been somewhere else. She was gnawing at her lips.

"Henry and Ruth Ann and I decided that somebody had to talk to you, and they chose me to talk for the family, for us."

"Now that we got it straight who the family is, what are you supposed to talk to me about?"

John Turner rose, walked to the picture window, and pulled back the curtains. "About that." He pointed to the backyard.

"About the *Cleo*?"

"Yessir, about that monstrosity, that boat out there."

"It is a *ship*, a Goddamned fucking *ship*, and—"

"Clyde," Cora cautioned, "your language . . ."

"The next one of you that calls it a boat can just get the hell out of this house and stay the hell out. You tryin' to make it sound like a toy, and it ain't. And it ain't got nothing to do with y'all, but since you've been elected family representative and all, go ahead and say what you got to say."

John Turner sat back down. "Well, we have decided that it is unfair for you to squander family money on foolishness like that b-b-b, that ship. We know it's your money, your retirement and

Social Security, but that money's supposed to see you through, to make life comfortable until, you know, until . . ."

Clyde stared at him. "Until I'm dead."

"Well, yessir. If you was to waste all your money on that big old barge, you know who'll have to come up with the money if you get sick and have to go to an old folks' home or get in bad debt or whatever."

At that Clyde stood up and reached for his hat. "Why don't you come with me, John Turner? I got a few things I want to say to you by yourself, since you are the spokesman."

The spokesman for the family looked at his wife, then stood up and followed the old man into the backyard. Clyde motioned for him to climb up the ladder behind him and onto the deck of the *Cleo*. He motioned to a nail keg. "Just set down right there, Son, and let me talk for a minute."

John Turner sat down, and his eyes swept over the interior of the *Cleo*, out of interest perhaps, perhaps out of dread.

"You just listen, now. I ain't going to say this but once, because to say it more than once would mean that I got some doubts about the truth of it, which I ain't, or that you ain't listened, which is your problem, not mine."

John Turner watched and listened without blinking.

"Hey, Grandpa." It was one of the boys, just over five. He had climbed the ladder and hoisted himself up onto the gunwale.

"Hi, Justin," the old man said. "Me'n your daddy've got some talking to do. Maybe I can bring you up here later . . ."

"Aw, Daddy, let him see the boat."

"John Turner, it is not a . . ." But he just let it slide. Nobody understood the difference.

The boy slipped between them and stumbled down some makeshift stairs into the cabin.

"You OK, Justin?" Clyde asked him, just as he poked his head out of the doorway and grinned.

"I fine. Bumped my head is all."

"Maybe you ort to go on back to the house. Me'n your daddy have got to talk."

The boy came up the steps and stood between the two. He looked seriously at his grandfather.

"What is it, Son?" the old man asked.

"What does *see-nile* mean?"

John Turner snapped forward. "Now, Justin, you'd better do as Grandpa says and go—"

"Naw, let him talk. Where'd you hear that word?"

"Well, Momma'nem was talking, and they said that you are *see-nile*. What does that mean?"

John Turner turned his head away from Clyde and looked somewhere far off.

"Aw, Justin," the old man said, reaching out and stroking the boy's hair. "They was talking about how me and your grand-momma are gonna go see the Nile. We gon' sail out of the Gulf of Mexico and across the Atlantic, that big ocean, and on into the Mediterranean and see the Nile. That's a river in Egypt. Weird one—it runs north."

The boy wasn't at all interested in the Nile and which way it flowed. When he looked through the kitchen window and saw his grandmother holding up a piece of cake, he scrambled over the side and down the ladder and they heard no more from him.

Clyde turned back to his son. "Senile, huh? Y'all are gonna *think* senile before all this is over."

"Before *what* is over? This damned shipbuilding business? Aren't you proud? I got it right."

"John Turner, you and the others ain't been much like family to us in quite a while. Y'all made it real clear a long time ago that you wasn't exactly proud to have people know that your daddy was a laborer in a shipyard. That's all right—I understand. And I can understand you not writing or calling or coming by except when you just had to, and not letting us be real grandparents to your kids. That has hurt like hell, especially your momma, but

I can understand it. What I flat-ass cannot understand is what right you got to tell me how to spend the money I have worked my whole life accumulating. Me and your momma sacrificed to raise y'all, sent two of you to college, bought you cars, give you the money for the down payment on your house. We done all for you that it was our duty to do."

He narrowed his eyes at John Turner.

"Now we got to do our own thing, as the saying goes. I got some good years left in me, and the money I been spending is mine, so you and the others are from this point on not to mess with me and your momma about the *Cleo*. I'm going to get'r done, and me and Cora are going to see the world in her. And if we spend every damned penny I have saved up over the years, that's all right too. I expect we'll sell the house, furniture, and everything else before we go, so that whatever y'all, the family, got coming will be in this ship."

The old man stood, rubbed his hand along the rail, which even before final sanding was smooth to the touch, and looked out toward the Gulf.

"When our time comes, y'all can come claim the *Cleo* and tug her back home, if you can find her and if you figure it's worth the effort."

John Turner, who had been leaning forward on the nail keg, hands on his knees, finally spoke: "Daddy, this is crazy. The neighbors think you're daft. Everybody in this town talks about Old Man McManus and his ark, and when they talk about you, they twirl a finger at their temples. The whole damned thing is embarrassing. It's ridiculous for a sensible man to be doing what you're doing."

"That may be, John Turner, but it's my backyard, my money, my time, and my Goddamned ship. So you let folks talk all they want to. Since you're the family representative, maybe you can explain it to them. Now let's get back to the house."

"I don't want to. There is more talking to do."

"Then stay your ass out here and talk to yourself. I am thoo talking." He swung over onto the ladder and went into the house.

John Turner just sat there a few minutes staring at nothing in particular, then got up and climbed down the ladder and went inside. In no time at all he had his family loaded.

As John Turner was driving away, he stopped, backed the car up, and got out at the curb. He turned to face Cora, who was still waving on the driveway. "You can tell him," he yelled, "that even if he does get that big piece of junk built, he'll never move it out of that yard! You just call me when you need us to come and tear it down and haul it off."

Except for occasional thinly disguised references to the *Cleo* by letter and by phone, the kids had little else to say about the project. John Turner told Cora on the phone one evening that they had decided to let the old man burn himself out on the boat. He assured her that they would look out for her if Clyde "wasted all the family savings on that junk of a boat." Cora told him that was real nice to know, then pointed out that it was a ship, and hung up.

Day after day, month after month, Cora watched Clyde disappear over the rail of the *Cleo* and descend into the depths, the hammering and sawing and banging punctuating her waking hours until whatever she did—whether cooking, sewing, or housecleaning—was done to the beat of the *Cleo*. She went out only when Clyde called her for help, preferring not to think about when the boat would be finished, if ever, and what changes would come into their lives if Clyde did fulfill his dream. She still thought of it as a boat, though she never said so to Clyde. A boat was something that never went anywhere much—a ship took to the high seas and went to exotic places. Except for the shifting around of scaffolding and the gradual disappearance of stacks of lumber, she could not tell that he was making any progress at all.

Then one morning, almost two years after the first stacks of timbers arrived, Cora looked out the kitchen window before breakfast to see Clyde applying a brilliant coat of white paint, and before the sun had set the next day, the ship was trimmed out in green and gold, as lovely and delicate looking as any ship she had ever seen. In another week the masts were up, the figurehead was mounted, and the name *Cleo* was painted on either side of the bow and across the stern. Clyde said it wasn't necessary to name her the *African Queen*, since any damned fool could tell from the figurehead that she was a queen and not a local one. And *Cleo* seemed so personal, so part of the family, like the name of a dog.

As the days progressed, there came plumbing fixtures, lights, portholes, lines, bits of teak and mahogany trim, and, then, lo and behold, one morning they walked out and stood before her in her resplendent glory: The *Cleo* was a ship, a beautiful little ship, anchored high and dry in a suburban sea.

After Cora's official tour, which left her breathless with admiration for such extraordinary craftsmanship in a man whose life work had been done for someone else and in the dingy dark beyond her sight, the two of them sat in lawn chairs Clyde had moved onto the deck.

"Reckon we look like the couple in the picture?" he asked her.

"I guess we do."

"It's finally finished. *Cleo* is real, she's ours."

"But what do we do now, Clyde? You're over seventy years old, and this ship is a long way from water. What do we do now, just look at her?"

"Let me worry about that. A little bit more varnishin' below and some riggin' to do, a lot of layin' in supplies and then. . . ." He sighed. "The world is ours."

Cora stared off toward the Gulf, where the sun was just losing itself to dusk.

"We don't know what in the world come of'm, John Turner." Mr. Burns, a next-door neighbor, pointed to the sign in Clyde's front yard. "All we seen was they had a FOR SALE sign in the yard for a couple of weeks, and had two big garage sales. Somebody brought in a big truck with a trailer and hoist behind it."

He pointed to the fence, where a large section was missing.

"Then we woke up yesterday morning and seen that SOLD sign and the boat was gone. He hauled it out of here at night— you can see where the ruts cut up the yard along the driveway— and they was gone. I called you soon as I could. Maybe if you had of come yesterday, you could of stopped him."

John Turner just stared at the tire ruts and gap in the fence.

"Mr. Burns, how could they haul a boat that big across the yard and down the street?"

"I don't know how he got that damned thing under the wires and all, without he lowered them masts, which is what he must of done."

John Turner still did not speak. He swept his eyes from the fence to the street, which led off toward the Gulf.

"Me and Molly drove down to the dock this morning, early, but that boat wasn't there. They done gone, John Turner. Furniture's gone, tools, cars. He sold everything and they done gone. He was sly about it too: Here one day, gone the next. But you know how your daddy is."

John Turner nodded and got in his car and drove off toward the landing, near the Coast Guard station, where they probably launched it. He parked and got out and walked to the end of the pier, then stood a long time and stared wordless out toward the Gulf, where, far beyond his sight, the grand ship *Cleo* sliced elegantly through water deep and green, while Clyde steered a steady course to the southeast and Cora sat in a lawn chair on the forward deck, a chart across her lap, studying the African coast.